Mei-Li is a first gen bod modder. They call her the Flesh-eaten Madame. She turned herself back when the new-anatomy fads first hit. Low tech body modification freaks were infecting themselves with bacterial agents back then. They wanted to reshape themselves, take control of their own anatomy. Bacteria were cheaper than going to the surgeons.

First Montag Press E-Book and Paperback Original Edition January 2015

Montag Press
ISBN: 978-1-940233-17-8
Cover art © 2015 Mariusz Siergiejew
Cover, layout, & e-book © 2015 Rick Febré

Montag Press Team:
Project Editor – Mara Hodges
Managing Director – Charlie Franco

A Montag Press Book
www.montagpress.com
Montag Press
1066 47th Ave. Unit #9
Oakland CA 94601 USA

Printed & Digitally Originated in the United States of America
10 9 8 7 6 5 4 3 2 1

the RED LIGHT PRINCESS

written by
JAMES W. BODDEN

MONTAG

the RED LIGHT PRINCESS

Chapter One
The Night of the Clean Hands

I look down in mid-jump, but can't see bottom.

My body hits the next roof with a drop and roll—legs tucked, turning round on my shoulder. They are catching up with me. I can feel them moving around in the dark: nothing but shadows, spreading out and trying to surround me.

I get on all fours. On bottom-feeder level. Crawling low to the ground to keep out of their line of sight.

The implants under my fingers heat up. I shoot an electromagnetic pulse through the launchers and jerk back with the recoil. A wave spreads out and boomerangs back to me, fluid like water. Everything it touches starts buzzing. Magnetic fields come alive. The contours of the roof are outlined by a crackle of vibration.

I can spot them now. Their bodies look shifty with static—old ghosts in my periphery. The fuckers are gaining speed and almost on me.

Morien pounces on my back and rolls me over. I try to buck him off—but he's stronger and has my throat pinned with his elbow. He flicks out his blades. The steel looms over me, points twisting from side to side, inching towards my eyeball.

I swallow hard, backing my head away from the blade. The shakes hit me again. A cold sweat splashes down my spine.

I try not to show it, but I can break easy. I'm not what I appear.

I've never been good at being a real man. Something's always been missing. I don't have the right tools and instincts. Give me a chance, and I'll run and hide to make it through another day. But there are worse things than being a coward. The drive's basic. My instincts are about survival. Cut and run.

I sweep my leg on the ground and trip him. Morien goes down flat on his face. I take my chances and gun it for the fire escape, but that animal of his is already on to me.

The animal walks circles around me. It sniffs the air, recognizing my scent. The outline of its back is muscular and bristled with spikes. It snaps its jaws at me. Hot saliva splatters everywhere. It lands a couple of bites, breaking through the skin. But I'm not feeling the pain. Morpho replica's got me numbed all over.

It lunges again, but can't get a hold of me. I'm too quick and manage to dodge and weave past it. The animal runs after me, mewling, getting desperate.

I'm about to reach the ladder, but have to backtrack. Sonya's blocking my way. She's got one eye closed and the other on the sights of her shotgun. The double barrels are locked on me. They've got me caught in her crosshairs.

I kick start the pedal on my talons, and spikes pop out from their soles. The pair of motorized crampons are implanted on my feet. They are braced around the ankle, drilled into the bones with a set of steel pins. I want her to know she's not taking me down easy.

"You're not shooting anyone. Not tonight." I meet her cold eyes. "There are rules."

Sonya cracks a smile, slick and red. She pumps the forestock of her shotgun and fires a load.

Buckshot sprays on the ground. I turn on my heel and run. Another round goes off. Debris sprays against my back. I pick up my pace and dive off the edge of the roof.

Skywalks spread all around me. A network of bridges connects the rooftops of the No Go Zone. They sprawl over the old high-rises and tower blocks forming a massive concrete hive—a teeming transit hub that orbits over the slums.

I blast another EMP. The wave bounces off the structures, mapping their grid. My implants are drawn to the metal buried in their foundations. Altitude, distance and angles are things I can reach out and feel without touching.

My body's with me. Every movement is controlled. I land on a bridge, hop the railing, and jump to the skywalks below it.

Wind cuts up my cheeks. My sweatshirt swells up like a balloon. I swoop down, knees bent, arms outstretched, and try to stick the landing.

I make my mark and pick up my pace, diving from one bridge to the next. Traffic is heavy. The skywalks are packed with bodies. I'm in the mix, moving among them, covering my face with my hood, blending with the crowd.

I'm just another street zombie, going about his night, inching on his way to nowhere. Nobody minds me. I'm nothing but ordinary.

There's no talent in hiding. A shift in posture can bring you down by a foot. Pulling out your face can age you. Never meet them in the eye. Go slight on your movements. Match the step of the crowd. Don't give them a reason to notice you, and you'll just disappear.

I look over my shoulder. They're gone. I lost them.

An electro-beat's stomping from the rooftops. The skywalks roar with noise. Crowds pack against the railings, riled and hooting, piling up into a mosh. Their clothes flap with the wind as they dance closer to the edge.

It's the Night of the Clean Hands, and the whole No Go Zone is in a riot. The festival's in full swing in every district. The roofs are jam-packed. Gamblers huddle in the alleys playing low-stakes games of dice. Stands and roll-away carts have set up shop on the bridges. They sell booze and meat charcoaled on the pavement.

The No Go Zone is in motion. It's alive and swept up by the night. This only happens once a year, and we all starve for it. One night without the fear of death doesn't sound like much, but it means everything here in the slums. Anybody would do something desperate to stay alive.

Everything goes on the Night of the Clean Hands: a night of freedom. A blank slate. Nobody has a past. We don't drink to the future. It's about the moment, betting everything on a whim because this will all be over when the sun comes up.

There are only three rules: Old debts are forgotten. Payback is forbidden. Killing is outlawed. But just for one night.

I tuck my rattail into the back of my sweatshirt and pull up the hood. There's a break in the crowd ahead. I find the nearest fire escape and take the stairs to the streets.

The queue on the fire escape is going nowhere. It's busy with the night's commute. Traffic is bogged and moving slowly.

I light a smoke and look up at the public viewing screens. They're huge and strapped on the backs of the tallest buildings on the blocks. The feed toggles with video coming from every corner of the No Go Zone.

Johnnie Manila's face pops on the screens, microphone in one hand and a pink drink in the other. His hair is slicked back, smile lubed with Vaseline. He's transmitting live from the Mecha Beast Wars again. Manila hosts the animal cyborg fights every year.

Humans used to play in the wars: bod-modders with weaponized implants. But they weren't able to cut it against the Mecha Beasts. They're badass killing machines. No human had a chance.

The ring is set up on a rooftop. It's covered in a chain link dome, topped with a row of spotlights and multidirectional cameras. The lenses zoom in on the fight.

Gorilla-xe is one of my favorite fighters. It's up in the ring now. The beast is in a rage. It swipes the axe heads surgically implanted to its arms.

The ape chases after a spotted cat. I can't quite make out what it is. It looks something like a leopard, but smaller. The tires on its front legs and the stilts in the back make it move in a slow trundle.

Gorilla-xe catches up with the cat and hacks it on the back, severing the power cables and then breaking the spine. Sparks go off. Blood cooks on the electrical wiring. The cat's hydraulic stilts keep kicking even after it is dead.

Johnnie Manila's snout pulls into a grin. Those bleached, oversized caps of his are the size of dump trucks, "Lynx 3.0 goes down… That twelve hundred PSI bite of his was good for nothing. Adios, motherfucker!"

Something's making the metal on my bones buzz. My implants almost anticipate it happening. Every screen fades to static. A hiss reverbs from the skywalks down to street level.

I stick my fingers into my armpits, trying to dull the sensation. My implants sting with the resonance. I feel the screech slicing through the air, hitting my bones with a low voltage.

One by one the feeds switch back on. The same image plays on the screens. A girl hangs from the belly of a skywalk. Her body swings with the wind currents.

The cameras zoom in on the girl's body. The rope around her neck rides up to the hinge of her jaw. A smooth, featureless mask hides her face.

She looks just like her.

Chapter Two
Dead Ringer

I hit the streets. They have a smoky, hermetic feel. Natural light rarely filters through to the lower levels.

Lampposts are on a twenty-four hour work cycle. They flicker from overuse. Bats fly in endless loops, unable to tell the difference between night and day. They go mad from exhaustion and dive on the pavement.

The No Go Zone is ungoverned territory: a black hole on the map. The high-density ghetto sprawls on the outskirts of the city limits on the other side of the separation barriers. The slums here fuse together into a solid block of construction, an unbroken urban landmass.

No cop's been spotted in the Zone for years. They learned to keep their distance. Last time they got inside the walls, they didn't last long. By nightfall their riot helmets hung off the skywalks like scalps.

You would think that there's anarchy in a place like this—chaos on the streets. But it never works that way. That's not the way the world works. Sure there is a bit of a storm out there. But things are measured; nothing goes out of bounds. Order always creeps in.

I was born and raised here. Never been outside the separation barriers. Don't know anything else. This is all I've seen. And I don't mind it. This world is good enough for me.

A motorized rickshaw flashes its lights at me. I run up

to the rear cabin. It's covered behind a curtain of aluminum privacy beads. My face multiplies on them like fly vision.

Mercury opens a gap in the beads. One eye is on me, gloomy like ink, "Get in."

I hop inside the cabin.

She doesn't say anything until the rickshaw begins to pull away. "You're late, Kai."

"What can I say? It's a long way down that rabbit hole." I grip the hydraulic pumps on her exoskeleton and run a finger up her instep. "I've missed you. It's been a while."

She shoves me back with her metal heel, "There's a reason for that. I'm the lone wolf type."

I try to remember our one-shot fuck, but can't picture a thing. Total blackout. The booze burned the night away. Now the memory's wasted.

Mercury's my boss. She's the eastern station chief for the 25's.

25 is triad slang for traitor. Our outfit is one of the most powerful in the Zone. The gang's banded out of a crew of triad rejects and deserters: men marked for their disloyalty.

One betrayal is all it takes. It's the first step to get initiated into the outfit. Each man who wants into the organization has to come clean and confess to an act of disloyalty. We all disclose in our crimes and share in the guilt. There's no bond like that of accomplices. You can't trust anyone until you've got something on them.

In a place with no law, it's the gangs and triads, the men with guns who become the new justice givers. There are always roles to play. And order always creeps in.

The 25's run District Five: everything from the arcades to the canals. Our information scavengers have the population here under constant surveillance. Every denizen in our district is tracked, movements filed in our registry, associations cross-referenced.

I'm one of them: an information scavenger, a human intelligence asset. I keep my ears close to the ground, scrounging out secrets, spying on the usual suspects and trailing every key piece of the No Go Zone.

Mercury plays a video on her console and flips the screen towards me, "We've got a dead girl hanging from the skywalks."

"Everybody's seen her. She's been playing on a loop on the jumbotrons." I pull off my hoodie. "You know how it goes. This place belches out bodies."

"Not tonight. The Night of the Clean Hands has rules. Old debts are forgotten. Payback is forbidden. Killing is outlawed."

"But just for one night..." I'm trying to charm her. My tone turns firm, steely. But this is not my voice. It's stolen from a better man than me. This is just another one of my small deceptions. Nothing comes naturally for me.

"We have our traditions here, Kai," she says. "A girl is dead in my area. Someone has broken the rules. I want the man responsible before dawn. A sacrifice is required. One man always dies so the rest of us don't have to. You know that better than most."

"I know it…" I mutter.

The Night of The Clean Hands is not without its price. Break any rule and the punishment is death in the ring. Every lawbreaker is thrown into the Mecha Beast arena to feed the night's champion. It's all done live on the public screens. The last act before dawn approaches, and the festival comes to an end.

The rickshaw comes to a stop. A large crowd is gathered

in the middle of the road. A guide ushers a pack of slum tourists through the street. They're taking pictures and pointing at the rope dangling from the skywalks.

Tour guides pay off the metro police outside the separation barriers to smuggle their buses inside. The tourists come here to window-shop poverty, looking to collect social trophies and share an experience from the margins. They're all trying to get a good view—owed their fair share of the spectacle.

I follow Mercury into the street. 25's are all over the crime scene, pushing back the crowd. We squeeze through and make it to the sidewalk.

The dead girl's body has been brought down from the rope and is lying on the curb. Buzzards fly circles around her. Smoke pushes out from their exhausts. The drones scan the body, recording video and capturing stills.

She's naked, skin bloated and gone blue with lividity. Her body's tattooed with a complex web of vines and rosebuds. Both her hands have been cut off. The wounds are fastened with a set of makeshift tourniquets: rubber hoses tied to pipes.

A cold wave beats from my implants. It spreads to the marrow in my bones. I take a step back. She looks exactly like her.

I know the answer already, but I ask anyway. "You got other informers working this district. Why'd you call me?"

Mercury grins with a mouthful of jade teeth, the latest fad in the Zone. "This case is made for you. This girl was killed just like her."

My chest puffs out. I pull back my shoulders and turn my back on her, but it's all a pose. I'm mimicking someone else's posture, and doing it badly.

I use my brother's voice again, "Don't bother me on a holiday…"

Mercury's exoskeleton runs up her legs and spine, spreading over her arms and totally covering her hands in metal. She grips my neck and squeezes. "There's nobody that knows about the murder of the Red Light Princess like you, handsome. You're one of her die-hard fanboys."

Her grip's a pincer; my windpipe closes. "The princess is dead. This girl is just an impersonator, a copy-cat corpse."

Mercury lets go and shoves me back. She traces the tattoos on the girl's stomach. "She's not the real deal, but she sure looks the part. The ink work is something else. Every stem and rosebud is there. Both hands are cut off below the wrist. Even the black pearls are genuine. She's a dead ringer."

A stick of tobacco dangles from my lips. I crouch over the body. My face reflects off the porcelain mask. "Big money is moving around the Mecha Beast fights tonight. This is gonna cost you."

"You're an information scavenger. You find out people's secrets and spill them for money. I know how much it takes for you to open your mouth."

"You know what they say. A man can make his fortune on the Night of The Clean Hands."

The mask is suctioned to the girl's face. It takes me a couple of tries to pop it loose. The girl stares straight at me. Her eyeballs are a crackle of veins. I take out my console and snap a picture.

I touch her lips. She's already cold. Her jaw's locked tight. I manage to pry open her mouth and slip my fingers inside.

Pressure builds up in my head. My skull's pounding. I'm not fully in control. My implants pick up every bit of resonance from the slums. Each pulse hits me in waves. They vibrate through me, heating up my implants.

I draw the jet injector from my holster, roll the cylinder to a vial of methadone replica, and give myself a full dose. I need the downer. The pressure eases. My nerves cool. The resonance fades.

I pull on my cigarette, "The tongue's been cut off."

"I told you," Mercury snatches my cigarette and steals a drag, "she's perfect."

"Does the girl have a name?"

"Her blood work came up positive. She's been infected with an HPV clone. Her pimps had her tagged. The sequencing code of the virus is registered to one of the brothels on the canals. Her name's Lin Kwong. She worked for the Shady Lady."

"What do you want from me?"

"I need you to go in. Sniff around and do your business. Track the girl's last steps. I don't want to know her whole story, just how it ended."

I cover the body with the mask, "Nobody's ever played dead like the Red Light Princess... But this girl could have fooled me."

"We have to be careful. These dead girls can get dangerous." The cigarette burns between Mercury's fingers, "The Red Light Princess's monks already go from street to street demanding fresh-cut limbs, burning entire buildings that refuse."

I nod at her and slip back into the crowd, getting lost with the tourists on the streets.

Chapter Three
The Separation Barriers

The free jumper's ribs are striped with grease stains. He arcs his back and stretches out the sails of a glider. Two spotlights glare under his wings. They attach to a cross-bar surgically bolted onto his back.

He jumps the railing of the skywalk and goes over the edge. The rest follow. His pack is modded with Omni-directional axial blowers, grappling launchers, and those new boosters everybody's going on about. The free jumpers hoot in mid-flight, shooting flares into the sky, trying to outdo themselves with high risk spins. Electromagnetic pulses shoot from the mirrored launchers on their fingers. Smoke trails from outdated, gas-powered propulsion packs.

I dive in after them—hit the next rooftop and try to catch up. The free jumpers move in a zigzag, maneuvering through a maze of cardboard tents. I pick up my pace and rejoin the pack. We launch off the other side together, a salvo of bodies.

Fuck the functional urban grid. Make your own. Free jumping is a new theory of motion. We are not rats running someone else's maze. Cities aren't just systems that control the way we move through space. They can be much more: free spaces that elude the formal structures of control.

There's a web of nets near the ground: safeguards for the jumpers. They're cushioned by a bed of refuse and broken furniture flung from the upper floors

I land on a fire escape and springboard to a ledge on the high-rise across the street. I'm always moving--dodging and weaving. Never slow, never stop and you'll just barley survive another day. It's all about staying alive. Basic, but true. Just making it through is enough.

The spikes on my crampons are out and drive into the ledge. They're fixed on the bones of my leg with pins and a steel brace. Two blades are attached to the toes. Six more jut from the soles.

I keep tic-tacking from one building to another until I reach the roofs. The separation barriers loom between the gaps in the high-rises. They tower over everything, casting a long shadow over the streets during the day. The walls are topped with a mesh wire fence and rows of outdated billboards.

The No Go Zone's in the ruins of the old world. We're squatting on someone else's abandoned infrastructure.

I shoot an electromagnetic pulse. Go as hard as I can— trying to extend my senses beyond the separation barriers. Cross the borders and catch a glimpse of the city by the bay.

My range is limited. But I can feel the warmth baking the stones on the other side of the walls. The magnetic fields out there are something else: super charged and revved with powerful sources of energy.

I've always wanted to see what is on the other side. Chase the sun, follow the spring and roll east.

There're ten magnetite implants imbedded inside my fingertips. Each metal component is fused to the bone. The micro-sensors are wired to my nerve endings and an external pulse launcher.

Human sensory modalities are outdated. They don't cut it here. The No Go Zone is rough terrain. Staying alive isn't easy. Scrambling on the rooftops can get dangerous. We need all the help we can get to survive.

My implants allow me to sense magnetic fields and feel the pull of metals. I can detect traces of invisible light, feel the slightest sonic shift like a bolt of thunder. Microwaves make an annoying crackle for me. High-tension power lines soothe me to sleep.

Magnetite implants are second gen augmentations: bio functional add-ons. But they're getting outdated by now. Third gen surgeons are already playing with new versions of biocompatible hardware and skeletal reconstructive surgery.

Progress seeps in slowly from the city by the bay. We get the tech scraps decades after they've already turned obsolete on the outside. Whatever wonders are out there are out of our reach. The tech gap is only getting wider. Fucking miracles are happening outside the separation barriers.

They tell me that I would not recognize the world outside. The light is overwhelming. Hovering ships cruise across their harbors. They've even changed the color of the water.

We're the forgotten people on the other side of the wall. There is no place else for us out there. They've driven us back and built the barriers to keep us out. The No Go Zone is our only haven left.

I take out my console and log on to the Casino Network. A new game of Five Card Draw pops up. The dealer hits me with a jack of diamonds, the ace of hearts and three random spades. I hold on to the spades and hope for a flush. The way I see it, I've been losing all morning and am due for a win.

No such luck, though.

I log off and start rifling through some old pics stored in my console. I find one of his photos and linger on it. Bale's arms are crossed over his chest. He's black-bearded, soot painted over his eyes. A thick braid runs down to his tailbone.

I flick at my rattail. It looks shriveled in comparison to his braid. We were never much alike. The man was hardened and battle ready. Bale was a real deal new world barbarian, a fearless fucker who never backed down from a brawl.

My rattail is no barbarian's braid. The thing is tightly wound, but flimsy at its core.

I'm not what was expected from me; never lived up to what anybody else wanted for me. I saw it as it was happening. It was a choice not to follow the path others had chosen for me.

But if he's disappointed in me, it's too late for Bale to show it. The tables have turned. I am my brother's keeper now--his memory, anyway.

I clench the cigarette butt with my teeth and scale down the side of the building to catch one of the ferries to the canals.

Chapter Four
The Three Sisters

The boat docks on the moorings. I hand the ferryman a fin and jump into the shallow end of the canals. The water goes up to my knees. It's black and swimming with dead rats.

I climb on the boardwalk and head over to the last brothel on the strip. Tourists are checking out the girls on the display windows. A man in a gasmask bumps into me. He tips his hat and crackles an apology from his respirator.

A crowd bottlenecks traffic near the Entrance to the Shady Lady. I try to get through, but the bodies won't budge. They're watching a troupe of dancers shake it by the entrance. The dancers are topless and wearing matching porcelain masks. I've seen them before: Red Light Princess Impersonators.

I scatter some loose change in their begging bowl, but they aren't worth it. The dancers got it all wrong. They're nothing like her—not even close.

I push the doors open and walk into the Shady Lady, one of the most expensive body modification bordellos on the canals. The hostess hooks her arms into mine as I step inside.

She spreads a smile that's all filed teeth. "What'll it be?"

I smile at her and tug at her nipple ring, "I'm looking for someone."

"You found her," she says, "if you can pay for it."

"I'm looking for someone special. Only the lady of the

house will do for me."

"She'd come apart like an old sack," the hostess laughs.

She leads me into the main room. All the booths have been taken. But I find an empty stool by the bar.

The bartender's double my size. His blunt, sloping forehead shines with sweat. He cultivates the Neanderthal look. The man's implanted with biocompatible Teflon and silicone. He's had rhinoplasty to flatten his nose and reshape his nostrils.

I ask for a beer and swig most of it down in a swallow. The music is loud. The bartender makes a joke about my gag reflex that I can't quite make out. I'd break the bottle over his head if I had any real balls.

My eyes scan the room. I get up and start nosing around the parlor. She's in one of the booths in the back.

The Madame shuffles a deck of cards, dealing herself another game of solitaire. Her body is covered in bandages. The dressings are spotted, but go mostly overlooked because of the lighting. Mei-Li doesn't see me coming.

I slip into her booth and smile broadly, trying to charm her, "It's been a long time, my old friend."

"You got that wrong." She comes out from the dark; her prosthetic nose is molded from rough pewter. "You're no friend of mine."

Mei-Li is a first gen bod modder. They call her the Flesh-eaten Madame. She turned herself back when the new-anatomy fads first hit. Low tech body modification freaks were infecting themselves with bacterial agents back then. They wanted to reshape themselves, take control of their own anatomy. Bacteria were cheaper than going to the surgeons.

She chose a cocktail of flesh eaters and leprosy. They say she was a sensation back in the day: cool and exotic — her exposed bones painted the color of mother of pearl. But that was another decade ago. Now's she's just outdated and falling apart.

Mei-Li keeps herself busy with the pack of cards, "What do you want from me?"

I touch her wet bandages, trying to fake closeness between us. "I'm here on business."

"You 25's are a bore…" she rolls her eyes, "not another interrogation."

"Have you gone outside tonight?" I ask.

"No, there's nothing to see out there," she says.

"I don't know about that. There's a dead girl hanging from the skywalks."

"You poor boy. You're strung out and getting flashbacks again. That princess did bad things to your head. "

"I saw the body. She's got the tattoos, pearls and everything. The girl looked just like the Red Light Princess." I tap the screen on my phone and show her the dead girl's picture.

"I can help you forget all about her." She points to the stage. "I have a whole host of horrors for you to wet your pecker."

Strippers slide down poles and spread themselves eagle on the catwalk. Their clits are beaded with colored light bulbs, the outer labia trimmed down or excised.

I clap at the performance and turn back to the Madame, "The dead girl's name was Lin Kwong."

"That doesn't surprise me. Those Kwong sisters were nothing but trouble."

"Sisters?"

"There were three of them: Lin, Shih and the little one, that one called herself Ana." She uploads a set of photos from her console into mine. "They came here looking for work. The girls were pretty, but they were clean: no implants or augmentations. They had no extra kink. I had them stick around, though. There's always the odd client who wants a taste of vanilla."

I look at their pictures. The sisters' resemblance to Red Light Princess was something else. "Good looking girls; you still got the eye."

She shakes her head, "It was a mistake to hire them. They were animals. Bad drunks and easy to violence. Those girls only made me money when they were passed out. They were out trying to make a name for themselves. The Kwong sisters were working on this Red Light Princess act on stage. They thought they were going to make it big."

"Were they any good?"

"They were something, to tell you the truth." Mei-Li collects her playing cards and stuffs them back in the box. "Specially the little one, Ana. That one had the princess down cold. But she couldn't be trusted. That girl kept things from me…"

"Where are they now?"

"Who knows? They've gone missing. The Kwong sisters skipped work for the last week."

A horned bod-modder is fucking a whore on the stage. He pulls out to show off his cock. The shaft is seeded with pellets of different sizes, ribbed to enhance the kink.

I finish my beer and spin it on the counter, "I need to find them. All I need is an address."

The Madam turns away from me, and I catch the outline of her pewter nose. "The last I heard, the sisters were living at the cage towers."

Her deck of cards is lying on the table. I reach for it, and she blocks my hand with her corkscrew fingers.

"What do you think you're doing?" Mei-Li asks.

My voice changes again. It rasps. The low husk is soothing and hints at seduction. "How about a game before I go?"

She chuckles and steps out from the booth. Her bandages are a tight fit. They ride low on her pelvic bone. "I'd eat you alive…"

Chapter Five
Density Rises

The cage towers teeter with the wind. They're built on the roof of every high-rise on the block. Steel housing complexes rise into the night sky like spires. Each single occupant pen is covered in mesh wire. Cubicles are mounted one on top of another and welded together into a rickety frame. The different levels are connected with a network of metal staircases that go around the outside of the structure.

I mix in with the crowds coming down from the stairs. The air's tacky. I can taste mouthfuls of sweat. I'm in the middle of a rush of traffic to the eastbound parties.

All the girls wear corsets and zippered minis. They got neon pigments injected into their eyeballs and never look up from their consoles.

Graffiti is scrawled on the ground: The same words repeated again and again, "Density rises. Still Alone?"

The No Go Zone is a high-density slum. We can't take another population explosion. Riots already spark like wildfire.

The commuters around me start to get restless. They are pushing and shoving back, bucking to get ahead. A fight breaks out a couple of floors up, and an old man gets tossed over the rail.

I climb the stairs to the upper decks. The cages get smaller the higher I go. There's just enough space for a miniature fridge, a bed and a piss tube that empties into a drain.

Migrants look at me from behind the bars. They're tanned, freshly arrived from somewhere shitty in the margins. In the city by the bay, the metro police hunt them down and dump them in truckloads through the separation barriers.

They come here because they can't afford the outside just like the rest of us. They are the outcome of urban displacement dynamics. Everyone wants to escape from the periphery to choke the center.

Space grows sparser every day. Migrant and native populations explode. Habitable space needs to be reinvented. There are other ways of inhabiting a city. Living space is the only real commodity.

I lean back on the railing and start a game of video poker on my console. The back of the digital deck of cards shows topless girls in Egyptian headdresses. I hit the deal button on the screen and they disappear, replaced by another lousy hand.

This has been happening all night. Every hand I play turns out to be a dud. Fuck it. I have to get back to business.

I head to the elevator running at the back end of the tower. The car operates as a mobile convenience store. It's stocked with loose smokes, booze, sweets and canned goods.

A patch of bleached hair is flat over my eye. My hood is up. I'm chewing on the butt of a cigarette. My pelvis is cocked to show off the guns in my holster, the jet gun and my snubby.

This could get ugly. I take out the snubby. It's an old school revolver with a three inch barrel. The caliber's nothing more than a pop. But it's got a sawed-off, hard boiled look that suits me.

I push the elevator's button with the barrel and the doors slide open.

Lucius Arseneaux's got his one arm crossed over the counter. It's oversized and tattooed with a circle of runic glyphs. His lenses slot out.

The spotlights on his headgear beam up at me, "Who is under that hood?"

"It's me." I uncover my face.

"No credit, only cash."

"You're not going to hold a grudge, are you, Lucius?"

He rolls out his wheelchair from behind the counter. His legs are long gone; the stumps are nothing but nubs. They barely inch out from their sockets near the pelvic bone.

Lucius Arseneaux is a believer; a Red Light Princess zealot. He has already given her most of his limbs and half an earlobe. The princess has her appetites. Her religion demands them fed.

"You owe me money." He wriggles the launchers on his fingers. "These magnets you sold me are nothing but a cheap alloy!"

"Take it easy. It's not like you're going free jumping anytime soon." I point down at his wheels.

Arseneaux pulls on a chain that opens a hatch on the floor of the elevator car. "You're lucky it's a holiday. I've thrown bigger men than you down this here shaft."

I smirk widely, "I hear the bones are piling up."

"Old debts are forgotten. Payback is forbidden. Killing is outlawed. I hate this fucking night..." He rolls back behind the counter. "It's pointless. Nobody here has any use for clean hands. This place is a wilderness. We're all beasts itching to draw blood by first light."

"Didn't you see the screens? Someone already did."

Arseneaux tugs on a lever, and the elevator pulls up to the top floor. "Had a good view, I saw her, trussed up and dangling."

"She remind you of anyone?" I ask.

"That wasn't right. Bad business to dress her up like that. Sacrilege." One of his goggles zooms in on the screen; the other retracts into the socket. "We already got ourselves our patron corpse. Don't need another."

"This new dead girl used to be one of your tenants when she was still breathing." I nudge the wheelchair back with my boot. "Her name was Kwong Lin. She lived here with her sisters. There were three of them. They were pretty girls: the kind a man like you would definitely notice."

"Never heard of them."

"I don't believe you." I fire a round with my snubby and burst one of his wheels.

Arseneaux flicks his tongue; it's gritty as sandpaper. "Dumb fucking rat, you think you're better than me just because you're four-legged. Look at yourself? That body of yours has no imagination!"

I pop the other wheel, "I'm warning you. Next one goes into your goggles."

"In a different time, boy, I'd have gutted you from throat to belly."

"But that was then... And this is all that's left of you." I point the snubby at his left socket. My tone shifts, becomes a steely baritone. I'm borrowing my brother's voice again. "Where are the Kwong sisters?"

"The Kwong sisters were insane. Believe me, I did us all a favor. We are all better off without them," Arseneaux says.

"I hear they had a reputation."

"You got no idea. These sisters were a pack of rampaging bitches. They used to practice their impersonator act on the sixth floor, naked as the day they were born, wagging those tight little tails, hooting this obscene mating call. It was a spectacle. Wasn't long before they started drawing a crowd. They lured those poor boys up there. Even the monks couldn't help themselves. Every night those sisters tossed corpses over the rails like leftover bones."

"What? You didn't get your slice?"

"Not even a taste." He rolls back, the flat wheels wobbling. "They barricaded the stairwell and started charging a toll. Those sisters played me."

"What happened to them?"

"They were behind on their rent. I sold them to the Eunuch. It took twelve of his men to hogtie the bitches down."

Good to know. The Eunuch will be easy to find. He's a big, wobbling target.

"Is that all?" I ask.

"I swear it by the mother," Arseneaux says.

"You're a believer, aren't you, Lucius? Do you perform the rituals? The amputations?"

"Do you see any extra limbs on me, motherfucker? I've made my peace with the princess, and it was a hell of a bargain. Give her enough body parts, and she'll make sure you never feel alone again."

"Why do you believe in her?"

"Because the Red Light Princess was real. I saw her myself." He points at his lenses, forming a tense V with his index and middle fingers.

I nod, "I know what you mean. The 25's thank you for your cooperation."

I cowl myself and turn to leave the elevator.

Arseneaux mutters something under his breath and jumps me. He bounces on his seat, bashing his metal headgear against the back of my head.

I fall flat on my face. The metal edges of the open hatch cut a gash on my lip.

I let out a cry. The cut stings. The taste of blood bursts in my mouth.

Lucius Arseneaux keeps my neck pinned with his out-sized arm. He's got his last working appendage jacked, the muscles veined and bruised. "A girl's dead on the Night of the Clean Hands. Someone's going to have to pay for her death by dawn. And the 25's aren't pinning this one on me."

My voice is my own again, weak and childish. All I can say is, "You can trust me."

Arseneaux laughs and pushes me down the hatch. My body goes into a tailspin. I'm hurling down and out of control. A cold pang goes up my spine. I grit my teeth and brace myself.

The drop's got me lost. Can't tell up from down. My body spins around, scuffing against the side of the building, spraying EMP's in every direction. It's all instinct. All I'm doing is reacting. My heart pumps against my ribs. I'm desperate for the feedback: some sense I'm still in control of where I'm going.

The wave boomerangs back to me, digging through my fingers to spark up with my implants. Vibrations map out the exterior of the high-rise. There's a break through the wall nine floors down. The opening is wide and rips across the midsection of the building.

I kick-start my crampons and I dig the blades into the wall to slow myself down. Sparks and bits of concrete ricochet around me. I'm closing in. My movements are timed. I retract the spikes just as I hit the mouth of the opening. My legs thrust into the break in the wall. I drop inside and roll on the ground.

My head hangs off the edge. I take in a breath. It's painful. My ribs feel cracked. I'm bleeding but can't figure from where. Sensation can get tricky for me. I get overloaded by my implants. There's a mess of nerve damage in fingers. I'm damaged goods. The implants have taken their toll and gotten infected twice.

I back up against the wall and take the jet-gun from my holster. I plunge the needle into the first vein I can find. The dose of methadone replica takes away all the pain. I've never had anything but a counterfeit high. Genuine narcotics and opioids are not available in the Zone. The real deal stays in the city by the bay. They say coastal cities always get the best drugs.

I get up and try to find the stairs. Trash burns in pyres all around me. My eyes sting, and the back of my throat's raw from the fumes. I keep close to the wall, trying to avoid the stink.

A mural of hers decorates the wall. The Red Light Princess sits in lotus position--one hand clasping a rose, the other a rope. Her body is covered in flowers and vines. A caption underneath reads, "Mother, forgive us."

The old girl can still pull an audience. People are coming in to kneel before her image. She's got her believers throwing fits on the ground. Women in veils clutch at prayer beads. Slum tourists stay in the back and take their pictures.

Boys with buzz cuts courtesy of the lice clinic light candles on the anniversary of her death. They're still novices, but already got the grey robes on. These boys will be monks soon enough. The first sacrifice in their training has been completed. They leave her an offering of severed toes piled at her altar.

I try to say a prayer for the princess, but don't remember how.

The back of the building is packed with a crowded shanty of tents and cardboard boxes. Every wall on this level has been torn down. The squatters have bulldozed through man-made barriers and the illusion of property rights, forming an open collective space. Property is all theft anyway.

Places like this are not supposed to exist, but they do. They are out there, and they are their own world.

These squatters aren't just aliens, drifters and undesirables. They're new world barbarians, conquering free spaces and making them their own.

My implants start buzzing. I feel the reverb of footsteps coming up behind me. Shadows warp and widen. They're running, picking up their pace.

I look over my shoulder, but can't see anything through the darkness. There's someone out there. I can feel it in my implants. Footsteps come up behind me.

A boost of adrenaline comes with the panic. I gun it for the stairwell. The stairs are packed. They've been taken over by a mob of dancers. Speakers blast from each end of the stairs. The dancers' palms are dipped in white chalk. They grind together and reach out to the ceiling. Girls work their hips in slow-mo. Replica dealers hand out vials and pocket handfuls of cash.

I elbow my way through and vault over the rails. The mob starts hooting as I drop. I catch the handlebar on the railing one story down and swing over to the floor below it, ricocheting from one rail to the next, until I land in a squat in the lobby.

I look over my shoulder again. My eyes dart from side to side. But there's nothing there. No one is after me. I feel silly. It's all in my head. Paranoia is a habit that lingers. I'm just a scared little man that doesn't want to get what he has coming.

I light up a smoke and go out the doors.

Chapter Six
The Mummy

I've been tracking him for a couple of miles, keeping to the roofs—the margins, out of his line of sight, jumping from one building to the next.

The eunuch makes a turn at the pedestrian crossing. He's big and easy to spot. His entourage keeps him slow.

He's surrounded by a cordon of bodyguards—Blue Lanterns: uninitiated triad muscle. His body slave holds up a metallic parasol that spins like a flying saucer.

Cyrus is an important man. He's the top-selling slaver for the Pale Horse Clan: the main triad in district three. The eunuch makes a lot of people money. He's untouchable. Shopkeeps sneer when he passes but take his cash all the same. Hard men talk trash to his back, though never to his face. He's not welcomed anywhere, but all doors are open to him.

I land on a tenement and slide down the roof's incline. My talons dig in for traction, tearing into the shingles. I break at the gutters and look over the edge. The eunuch and his men stop at the next street corner. They're waiting for the bull to make its pass down the road.

The bull is bolted together out of the chassis of some lurching, prehistoric tank. It's covered with skins and rawhides. The head is fresh-cut. It hangs on the end of the barrel.

That thing comes out every Night of the Clean Hands. It runs laps around the districts of the No Go Zone until it runs out of gas at dawn. The bull puffs a thick cloud from its exhaust and makes a turn around the mausoleum on the other side of the street.

The eunuch crosses over and says a prayer before he goes into the crypt. Only his body slave follows him inside. The Blue Lanterns stand guard at the gates. They stop every pretty girl who comes close for a grope and a pat-down.

I bounce off the gutters, jump over the street, and land smack on the dome of the mausoleum. The marble is wet. My crampons are having trouble holding on to the red stone.

My console's in my back pocket. I take it out and tap on the snarfing application. The Jolly Roger icon turns on the screen while it buffers and searches for other mobile devices within its reception range. The Snarfer lets me siphon digital data off encrypted devices, copying the information into my console for analysis.

I press the skull icon, and the crossbones go red. My mobile syncs up with the eunuch's. The program breaks through his safety settings and cracks every single one of his codes. I'm in. I dig through his folders and find the documents: his books, the daily inventory. The files are downloading. The app's skull goes yellow and turns on its axis.

My body is flat on the dome. I'm on bottom feeder level again, skulking around, out of sight, moving in darts. Data scavenging is all about the wait and the scud. Bide your time. Leech as much information as you can carry. Keep out of sight and run the first chance you get.

This is taking longer than I thought. I reach into my pants for a smoke, but the pack comes up sideways and gets wedged in my pocket. They're caught tight.

I look at my console. The Jolly Rogers does nothing but spin. It's taking too long. The wait's killing me.

My implants start buzzing. They're picking up movement. But there's something else. I am being traced with beams of light. I can feel the heat dotting my back.

I look down the edge of the dome. The Blue Lanterns crawl up the walls of the mausoleum. A few of them are already on the dome. They point their laser aims at my back. One of them starts barking orders to put my hands over my head.

I try to jump and make a break for the roofs, but my crampons slide on the wet marble and I lose my grip.

My body crashes down on the sidewalk with a thud. The Blue Lanterns surround me in seconds, guns pulled and aiming at my head.

Cyrus stands at the gates of the mausoleum. His cheeks are plump and have a butter shine. "Take this rat inside. My girl could use the company."

"Hi there, eunuch." I smirk and wave at him.

"Is it not better to be men like you and I, men who call things by their real names?" he asks me.

"I don't know about that. My tongue can get me into trouble."

He's amused, his belly shakes, "You poor fool, you don't know how to use it. There is no deadlier weapon. Better than a knife in the back."

His men toss me into the crypt. I roll on the ground and thud against the legs of the casket.

The Eunuch moves in small, feminine tiptoes. His body slave keeps two steps behind him, following tradition. The boy's been waxed and scented with oils. He's shackled by the neck, and Cyrus holds the leash.

"You're interrupting," the eunuch says. "I have a date

with a girl, Kai."

"Have you ever touched a live woman, eunuch?" I cough out blood with my spittle. Red specks cling to the glass casket.

"I used to be the terror of the body modification bordellos." His legs rustle as he walks; the meat grazes and slaps with every step. "But it was all for the sake of appearances."

"Does your date know about that?" I nod at the corpse in the coffin.

The Red Light Princess lies inside the bulletproof glass casket. Her mummy's fitted into a flesh-toned zentai. The rubber hugs tight to her body and outlines the groove of her bones. She's got no hands. The gloves lie flat at her side.

She's been mummified through plastination: her body preserved with injections of silicone and liquid plastic. A featureless mask rests over her face. The porcelain reflects the red dome.

I walk up to her. My hands streak the panes. She looks small, flimsy like a rag doll. I get in close enough for my breath to condense on the glass.

I have the impulse to lever open the casket and snatch the mask off her face, make sure she is what she seems. "The princess was something else. Wasn't she? That girl had the whole Zone in a trance. She was the most beautiful thing we had ever seen."

"I don't know about that, Kai." Cyrus tightens the sash on his yellow robe. "Men see beauty wherever they can get it. But that's the allure of the Red Light Princess. Like any good whore, she was whoever you wanted her to be."

A ring of torches at the foot of the dome light the burial chamber. My shadow is cast over the body of the princess. I'd like to offer a prayer for the dead. But don't remember how.

"Do you want to hear a story?" Cyrus's voice sounds sweet

and pleasing.

"Not tonight…"

"I wasn't talking to you. I was asking her. The princess always liked a good story." The eunuch snakes around the casket, cooing to the mummy inside. "You were born to slum land royalty. Your father was one of the big boys. His gang was a strong one, it ran everything from district seven to the southern separation barriers. Back then, Hannibal was a man to be feared. He believed in the old ways, the forgotten traditions. For a long time, before he lost his mind, he offered the sacrifice at the end of the Night of the Clean Hands. And the people loved him for it.

He shakes his head, coyly, trying to tease her, "You were a bad little number and took to the pipe early. The cards came next. They say you were trained for pleasure since before you could bleed. It was no surprise when you ended up in the brothels.

"Hannibal knew you were trouble. Only bad things could come from such a pretty girl. You were made for temptation. You would be a source of jealousy and greed. Men would lust, plot and kill to claim you as their own. He decided to place you in the public domain and donate your body to the pimps as a gift to the people.

"When the pimps saw you, they knew they had something special. They branded you as the most expensive tail in the No Go Zone: a woman almost out of any man's reach. They made you a star.

"But you became something larger. Your following grew. You transformed into a slum tourist attraction. My girl, you were famous. You were on the graffiti on the separation barriers. Girls went to the surgeons to bring them down by a foot to match your size. Transvestites working the strip were playing you right on the money. Impersonators and fake web cams were everywhere. Men started praying to you, begging for a taste. That legend of yours spiraled out of control. You gave the people hope. They were told you were all they ever needed.

"You loved the touch of the sun and took long strolls on the skywalks near dawn," he sighs. "Poor girl, you never saw it coming. It happened on another Night of the Clean Hands. Our laws were supposed to keep you safe. But death was out there. And it was stalking for you. Killers cornered you in the skywalks and went at you with knives. Your hands were chopped off. Tongue ripped from your throat. They took you apart piece by piece and hung you by the neck for everyone to see."

"I think she's heard this one before," I snicker.

We face off across the princess's casket. Cyrus drums his fat fingers on his belly. The buzz goes that the eunuch has a full castration job, seeds and stem rooted out for the Red Light Princess.

"What were you doing skulking in the roof?" he asks.

"I was just passing through."

"No. No. No. You're a 25. Your kind never just passes through." He whistles and the body slave hands him my console. I must have lost it in the fall.

I draw my snubby, point it at his belly and borrow my brother's voice again, "I don't want any trouble."

"What do you think you're doing with that barber shop toy? It won't even cut through my first roll of fat."

He tosses the console back to me. The screen's cracked, and the Jolly Roger is still spinning. I try to log out, but the app isn't responding. This always happens. I shut down and reboot.

I light up a smoke and keep the voice. It makes me feel bigger, stronger. My ribcage expands. Jaw slots out. "I'm looking for three sisters. They were sold to you last week. I'm sure your stock's overloaded with cunny, but these girls would have made an impression."

"The Kwong sisters," he smiles.

"Fuck me. These girls are getting famous."

"Take my advice; walk away from this. Those girls aren't the kind you want to get mixed up with. They are not playing around."

"You aren't scared of these girls are you, eunuch?"

"They look just like her. Aren't you?"

"They're just impersonators."

"You're wrong, Kai. These sisters are much more. They could draw a crowd. They are all beautiful and dangerous, but it's the littlest one who has got the hidden talents. She caught my eye early. She was something else. That girl was a boy. She was waxed, nails manicured, cock expertly tucked back and taped, the curves of the hips reshaped by binding the bone. That boy plays the princess better than anyone I've ever seen. The crowds would've loved him."

"Where are they now?"

"The Kwong sisters were getting a following. They caught the attention of the monks. I found a buyer for them this morning."

"Check your files. Who bought them?"

"My console is just a decoy. I don't keep electronic re-cords anymore—too many rats out there scavenging for data." Cyrus yanks the chain and tugs his body slave to him. He taps on the boy's buzz-cut head. "Everything important is in here. He has a mind like a machine."

I run the barrel of my snubby up the body slave's stom-ach, "Does he talk?"

"If you press the right buttons," the eunuch says.

The boy's voice comes out fast and mechanical, "The monks paid fifteen hundred cash plus an additional one hundred as a fee for the costs of sedation and shipping. The packages were transported under refrigeration, vital organs in full working condition, to the delivery address: the top floor of the Paradise Hotel."

I cock the trigger, "Anything else?"

"They said they were taking them to the big man: the preacher, Hannibal."

I turn back and head for the gate, but the eunuch calls me back.

"These sisters aren't the only reason you're here, Kai." He traces his hand over the glass casket. "You wanted to see her, didn't you?"

"I don't know what you mean."

He sidles up behind me, his breath on my neck, "Don't bother lying to me. You were hypnotized by her just like the rest of us. The princess meant something to you too. You wanted to see her again. You miss her too. The princess lures us all like flies. You are just like the rest of us, and can't let her go."

He's toying with me—wants to see me react. But I'm stone. I'm owning this moment. He won't see anything but what I show him.

"She's been dead for a while," he says. "We're going on five years now. But no one has forgotten that night. It changed everything. I could hear them screaming for miles. Lovesick boys threw themselves off the roofs. Thousands lit candles at her vigil. Monks turned their back on their old religions that night. They exchanged them for something real. We all came out into the streets to watch her hang."

I pull from my cigarette's filter, trying to look cool and in control, "I remember…"

"Her murder cast a spell on us. Nobody could let go. The princess was too special. She was famous. We all thought she would always be with us." Cyrus snakes around me. "Her murder was never solved. Nobody found her killer. That sort of stuff feeds people's imaginations. It was the mystery of it. That was the needle. It got us hooked on her."

"She always was a good drug," I say, "Who knows what happened? There are so many stories out there."

"And I've heard them all. Some say the princess was hit by a metro police cleansing squad. There's also the one about her owing a fortune to the triads. Or the story about her jealous transvestite body double. But that's just feed for the tabloids."

"It's always the same when celebrities die. Everyone has their own conspiracy theory. Take your pick. Nobody's ever satisfied."

"Why would we be satisfied?" he asks. "Death doesn't end our devotion. It only makes it stronger. The princess means more to me just because she's dead."

"That girl has done things to your head."

He pats my back, "Don't pretend she's not crawling inside of yours."

He's got that right. I know what he means. There's an air of mystery and longing that I've only felt from the dead.

I step out of the burial chamber, close the mausoleum's gates with a clank, and watch bats scurry from their perch on the dome.

Chapter Seven
Order Always Creeps In

Buzzards fly above me in the night sky. The drones move in a triangle formation. Their lenses tape the activity of the crowds below. One of them slows down, extends its camera, and sets its eye on me.

I keep to the roofs, jumping from one tenement to the next, headed for the Paradise Hotel.

There's no electricity or running water in this sector of the No Go Zone. Sewage overflows on the streets. The roads are dangerous: a high risk infection area. But the people here make do. They self-organize and survive. The squatters have made their own world for themselves.

Women hang laundry from clothing lines fixed between the buildings. A group of day laborers on the roofs collect rainwater from a set of plastic drums. Poachers track a flock of pigeons and swing their nets. They carry off their catch to sell at the micro markets that operate on the different housing projects on the block.

Every building here has its own market and its own rules. Some share their resources. Others barter and trade. But most of them are run by the native No Go Zone franchises.

The No Go Zone chooses its own path. Dense, disorderly and overwhelming, it is a pirate land grab. The colonial drive to plant our flag on someone else's land is now ours.

I decide to take a break and sit on the edge of the roof.

A gust of wind hits me and sends my rattail flapping over my shoulder.

I pull out my console and log on to the Casino Network. My first hand's a low payout: two measly pair. I hit the deal button again, and a warning message pops on my screen. My account's daily three-hour gaming run has expired. I'm locked out of the site. The city by the bay's government anti-addiction fatigue system has kicked in.

A fucking government mandated shutdown. Our play-time is monitored. Governments always try to regulate vice and cyberspace. Both are unbound and their pull is strong. This foolishness is doomed to fail.

Those men and women that live in that city outside built the separation barriers; they all wanted to keep the undesir-ables out. Keep the margins contained, away from the center. Keep themselves nestled and safe. But we don't get the same courtesy. They don't keep to their side of the wall. It's them and their tourists and their rules that sneak in our way. Their order always creeps in. It seeps through the cracks in the walls.

They say the No Go Zone is the last free spot on the globe: an anarchist haven. But I don't believe a word of it. The government is in the chlorine in the water. They creep across air and digital space. They're all-terrain now. We're still connected to their grid.

I play with my snubby's trigger. Old and rusted, its reflex-es aren't what they used to be.

My implants start buzzing. I look over my shoulder. There's something out there, breathing down my neck.

Pickpockets. They're hiding in the dark, unlit patches of the roof, skulking about on their haunches. Lean and oiled, the slippery fuckers are naturals in the shade. Their hands are tiny. The younger boys bind them early to keep them small and stealthy. They inch closer, getting ready to pounce. Drag me into a dank corner. Strip me naked, bring out their scalpels, and scavenge for my choice internal organs.

We're all on a chase here and there's no sole hunter. Every one of us is closing in on the other. And we all have to look behind our backs to avoid getting what's coming to us.

I draw my snubby and fire a warning shot into the air. The pickpockets scatter.

I'm going the wrong way. The southbound skywalks are up ahead, but I should be headed north. I take out my console and punch in my location. The navigator analyzes the coordinates and charts a path over the roofs. The route will keep me on the upper levels. No need to touch solid ground.

The key jump points flash with arrows on the screen. I'm supposed to take the skywalks until I reach the helipads on forty-second street. Take a turn at the crossings and follow the tenements to the end of the block. Then it's a ten-story drop to the morgues, and The Paradise Hotel should be right in front of me.

I cross over to the other side of the bridge. Something's off. I can feel it through the magnetite discs hotwired to my nerve endings. It starts as a static, then a low rumble of noise. It's getting louder, rising. There's a rush of movement under my feet. I lean over the railings to check out what's going on down there.

It's just bats. They're flying in circles around the foundations. The animals are mewling, rebounding off each other, fighting for space. The flap of their leather and fur makes me cringe.

My instinct is to dull the sensation: drown out the sound, self-medicate. The jet gun's already in my grip. The needle grazes against my neck, trying to find a sweet spot on the jugular.

"That won't do a thing." There's a voice out there. "When you come back down, you'll still remember everything you've done."

I stop and look over my shoulder.

There's a bag lady huddled by a cook fire. She's hidden under a trash bag poncho. It spreads over her like a tent.

The bag lady shuffles under her plastic coat, craning her neck, straining to make a connection with me. I avoid her eyes and try to sidestep around her.

"Where do you think you're going?" she asks.

"Don't piss around with me. I got work to do."

A shotgun slots out from the trash bag poncho, "You're not leaving me again"

I try to turn back and run, but she knocks my wind out with the barrel. I hit the ground on my hands and knees. My stomach's empty. Nothing but a wad of acid comes out.

My eyes dart from side to side. I got them clocked. Morien crawls up from the belly of the bridge. His animal jumps from an unlit patch of the deck and comes at me.

The albino Doberman is a designer breed. The size of it is unnatural. The dog is a result of generations of experimental incest. It's a genetic abomination, cursed with a photosensitive hide and a quick temper.

The dog comes straight at me. I turn to run, but the animal bites into my leg and drags me through the deck like a rag.

I manage to pull out my snubby. The albino glares down at the sawed-off barrel with a spark of recognition. It releases my calf and backs away next to its owner's side.

It's been a while, but I'd recognize him anywhere. Morien's walking on all fours, legs on their haunches, fists firm on the ground.

There's something different about him. I can see his bones pop from under his skin when he breathes. His ribcage extends down to the navel and goes around the sides to cover the lower organs. The torso looks ribbed and fully armored.

I snake around him, trying to check out his body alterations. He's jacked with third gen body modifications. New prosthetics have been filtering in from the city for a couple of years now, but you don't see much of it out there. It's still in its beta stages. The fad hasn't mainstreamed.

It seems wrong, something alien, but I like it.

Only a couple of surgeons have the right equipment for this type of custom work. He's had a full skeletal rebuild. The bones on his arms and legs have been extended. Every anchor point is moved away from the joints for stability and an enhanced jump. The prosthetic bones are lighter. They make him flexible, give him better maneuverability.

This is dream free jumping tech. He looks sleek and ergonomic. The things I could do with his body race in my head. I would streak through the sky. Fast. Nothing could stop me.

I look down at my talons. The spring mechanisms are getting rusted and they creak when I walk. I feel outdated here.

Morien's changed his hair and cut it into tawny spikes. A ginger braid runs down to the middle of his spine. My rattail looks wimpy by comparison.

"Loki's been shot before." Morien scratches the albino's head. "He knows a gun when he sees one."

"Why do you still keep that mutant?" My leg throbs.

"He's family, Kai. Loki was the only sane one out of the entire litter. This one always backs down from a fight he can't win. The others were tougher. They were brave fuckers. But they all died early."

Sonya shuffles off the trash bags on her back. Her heels slip and tack on the deck. She's fitted with her second skin, a pelt stitched with furs and a striped rawhide.

They look straight at me. I can recognize them, but there's something off about the way they appear. It has been too long. This all feels familiar, but it's unreal. It looks like it should, but something is still wrong somehow.

"What are you doing here?" I get up from the ground.

Sonya sweeps a blond braid away from her face. "I'm here to see my son."

"It's been a while…" I don't know what to do with my hands, so I reach out to her, touching her arm.

Her body stiffens, and she steps back slowly.

"You meant the dead one… Are you still in mourning?" My hand slides off her, running down the pelt. "You do realize he doesn't have a grave. We never got any of his pieces back. There is nowhere to go to grieve him."

"That doesn't matter. A mother's mourning is always long," she says.

This is my old pack. We share blood and bad history. Just like any other family, there's an old debt standing between us. I know it already. They're here to collect.

Sonya's face is still pretty, but it's grown stiff and joyless. "This place is a tomb. No soul can get out. How can you live like this, buried alive without seeing the sun?"

"We get used to what we have to. Eat a little bitterness. It's the way a man survives," I shrug. "When did you come back?"

"Morien drove through the city by the bay like a bat out of hell. We crossed the separation barriers at nightfall," she says.

"What's it like on the outside?" I ask.

"You wouldn't believe what's out there, brother." Morien's lips split with an impish grin.

Sonya moves closer to me. Her furs double her size. "We can't help but follow the road on the outside. We squat and live off the land. Scavenge and steal only what we can carry. Keep only what we can hold. It's in our blood. Our ancestors were drawn by the pull of the horde. We are the new world barbarians."

My mother calls us new world barbarians. She thinks we are the heirs to the wandering tribes, the hordes of the frozen steppes and the old Khans. We are the outsiders: wanderers and urban rangers. Savage and deadly, bashing against the gates of civilization.

My tone grows grizzled. It's on to my dead brother's frequency. "The same old story…. I've heard this one before. Nothing has changed with you."

Sonya's eyes are ice. They move over me like slow glaciers. I know those eyes well. They are my own. "You've stolen his voice, but it fits you badly. Bale was nothing like you. My son was strong and fearless. That boy respected blood. He was loyal."

I can't hide my embarrassment. My face rushes with blood. I feel small and found out.

"How many times do you want me to say it?" I mutter, "We got no score to settle between us."

Sonya shakes her head, "No such thing as even, Kai."

"There's no going back now, I say.

"Is it so easy for you?" She glares at me from the corners of her eyes. "Have you forgotten everything already? You owe me!"

"I remember." I kick start my talons.

Morien starts walking circles around me and tugs at my rattail, "What are those supposed to be? Two rat traps strapped on your feet?"

"Want to try them out?"

"You never had the balls to stab someone up close. Never face-to-face. The backstab is all you know."

Morien pulls me back by my rattail and slams my face against the railing. I wipe the blood from my nose and look over the edge. The bats bash against each other, ballooning into a black cloud at the foundations of the bridge.

"Isn't this nice? Just like old times." Sonya looms over me.

It's getting hard to keep it from them. I got the shakes again. My implants beat under my skin. I've never been good at fighting. My instincts only tell me one thing: run.

Morien's forearms are wound like trunks. The skin looks spotted and scarred. Black stitches crisscross up to the nook of his elbow.

The stitches start to pop loose. The skin splits open and a large metal slab slips from the fresh gash. Its edges are serrated and fold out from the hollow between the bones in his forearm.

My implants start buzzing again. They pound, hot and urgent. I feel it in my gut. Every magnetic instinct that I have developed tells me to get down and duck.

I hit the floor just as his scythes pass over my head.

Morien swipes his blades at me again. I bring out my talons and parry them away with a kick.

Angry lines crawl at the sides of his mouth. He goes at me, full strength. I manage to dodge away from him. His blades hit the ground and he screams out.

I see him shaking from the pain of the metal hitting the concrete. He must feel that aching on his bones.

I jump over the railing and dive, swooping through the cloud of bats. The animals flap around me, nipping at my heels, sucking on my skin, honing in on my body heat.

Chapter Eight
Another Mirage

I jump the ledge with a back flip. My core's tight, arms extended for balance. Each electromagnetic pulse makes me feel like I'm displacing salt water.

The landing's a hard one. My ankles take the hit. The pins that brace the talons to my leg put pressure on the bone. I have to keep going on all fours for a while to relieve the pain.

My console starts beeping. The last jump point is up ahead. It's at the end of the roof. I dive off and make the drop to street level. My body rolls on the sidewalk, shoulder to heel and up on my haunches.

The street ahead is nothing but morgues and ash holes. Every columbaria on the block is advertising short-term leases and family combos.

The sidewalks are packed with mourners waiting to claim their dead from the morgues on the strip. They've been there waiting for days. The morticians can't handle the business. Bodies keep piling up inside their fridges. The doors can't close all the way. The dead ooze on top of each other— nothing keeps.

Tradition in the No Go Zone is that the dead must be burned. Space here is limited, the population already densely packed. The departed have to give way for the living.

Fresh corpses are being delivered in rickshaws. A new batch of bodies has fallen from the skywalks. They are piling up on the street, waiting for the furnaces.

It happens every year. Teens, boys, and girls kill themselves on the anniversary of the Red Light Princess's death. They want to give it a shot: make it big, replicate in her fame. But it never works. They are all cheap copies and every one of them is forgotten.

There's a woman staring at me from a queue across the street. She's got black holes in her eyes. They're sucking me into their sockets.

She's clad behind a sequined burqa. It's beaded and embroidered around the hem. Two little girls in identical garments hold her hands.

The veil flaps across her, and I see the princess's face. With each ripple of fabric, she changes. The woman morphs from one Kwong sister to the other. Lin's covering her face with the porcelain mask. Shih's got the rope over her neck. Ana calls back to me. They're all screaming.

My head starts pounding. The people walking on the street. Noise from the windows. The speakers on the skywalks. It's all a cloud of noise. My implants are overloaded, picking up every bit of resonance from the slums. Each pulse hits me with an electric shock.

I can't take this woman's gaze. There's something about her. She looks like she knows too much. I try to hide, mixing in with the crowds. My shoulders are hunched, knees spread out like a crabs. I look shorter, a heavier man using my same sweatshirt.

But she's still following me. The woman won't break our connection. She's melting the ice in my eyes.

What does she see when she looks at me? There's more inside of me than meat, bone, wires and metal. There's fear and violence under the surface. One always follows the other.

I can't keep calm. My breath's gone short. The paranoia bubbles inside of me.

This woman is just a mirage, a trick of the eye. Just like me. This is the No Go Zone. Nothing here is real.

But I can't help it. She looks real to me. So I draw my snubby and aim it at her face.

She freezes for a moment. Her head is shaking. I have to cock the gun to snap her out of it. The woman clutches her daughters and runs.

I lean back on a lamppost and watch the crowd drift past me. My jet gun's pressed against my neck. I stick the needle in, trigger the plunger, and pump in a vial of morphine replica. It's good. I moan loudly as it hits. Cock tents out with a semi. There's nothing like it. Not even close.

Chapter Nine
The Preacher

The Paradise Hotel is up ahead. I walk into the lobby, and a cloud of dust lifts behind me. The floor is stripped to the bare cement base. It's been mined for the iron rods and marble.

Back in the day this place used to be the tallest ash hole on the strip. It was expensive. Rent doubled by the floor. The penthouse suites offered mourners balconies, skylights and hourly servings of complementary tea.

But it went out of business years ago. It's been abandoned ever since. Such a waste of space. This building used to mean something. It was a status symbol. It meant you would not be forgotten. The professional wailers made sure your ashes would always be mourned and remembered. Men paid small fortunes to be buried on a floor closer to the sun with round-the-clock mourners bawling at their graves.

There are not many places like this left in the No Go Zone. Open, wasted spaces, free for the taking, an entire building that hasn't been occupied. Not even the new migrants will squat here for a night. This place has been marked. The dead have left their stink on it, and everybody has their superstitions.

I press the buttons for the elevators just for kicks. They are out of order. Every car has been pulled out from the chutes. They're crumpled and turned over, strewn across the lobby.

My implants start buzzing. The lobby's doors swing

open, and a gust of wind blows cold across my face. I can hear steps coming up behind me.

My eyes swivel from side to side. Heartbeat races. I scud into one of the elevator cars and hide inside, pulling up my hood, going into a fetal position, making my body into a compact ball.

An old woman crosses the length of the lobby and heads for the emergency stairs. Her face is covered with a veil. Prayer beads roll between the palms of her wrinkled, fingerless hands.

I slip quietly out of the elevator car and follow her.

It's pitch black in the stairwell. Not much light filters down. I scrunch my eyes and fumble around in the dark.

I shoot an EMP and scan the stairs. Rats bristle at the vibrations. They're running scared and scudding back into their holes.

I keep my distance to stay out of sight, low on the ground, on the edges and black spots of the stairwell. Back against the wall, scuttling like some low vermin. On bottom feeder level. The world down here is smaller, compact and all my own.

There's a slew of engravings scrawled on the steps. Mourners have chiseled the names of their dead and left them messages on the concrete. I stop midway to finger the inscriptions, mouthing the names without speaking them out loud.

I follow the old woman to the top floor of the Paradise Hotel. The walls are covered with rows of empty burial niches. Their numbers have been scratched off. Black wasps have built hives in the holes.

Light comes from the back of the hallway. The old woman is drawn to its magnetic pull. She follows it like a signal, moving closer to the source.

I'm working a light sweat, hiding behind one column and then crouching behind the next, staying out of sight. The obstacles keep me sharp.

The old woman joins a crowd of fanatics gathered close to a pile of burning tires. I cowl myself and mix amongst them. A painted whore from the canals goes into fits on the floor. Rural migrants bow their heads and huddle together. Cultists from the upper communes play nervously with a high-powered rifle. They're pale and shirtless, backs whipped to the bare flesh.

The smell of blood gets me first. I only notice the puddle after I step into it.

The monks are in the back. They chant and heat up their instruments on the fire. Every one of them is missing a piece of his original anatomy. Fingers, hands, noses and toes. They looked chewed on. Used. All holes, black stitches, pus and scar tissue.

A queue of believers circles around them. They're waiting in line to give the princess her alms. The monks chop off the choice body parts and toss them into a pile.

I spot Hannibal behind the fire. The crowd's getting thicker the closer I get to him. I'm weaving through the mess of bodies, inching closer.

The old man hasn't lost the look. He's still mean and hardened. Hannibal's chest is powerful. His chinless head rests on a pair of sturdy shoulders. He wears a simple sackcloth tunic. The grey material looks moth-eaten, and the threading comes apart at the seams.

The preacher and his sons were fucking famous. They had their own slum land ballads. Their giant faces were on the graffiti on the alleyways. Their gang fought at the sack of the Burned Market. Hannibal lost all of his sons in the firefight with the triads. He took out every Red Pole himself, dislodging their jaws. The old man went up on the skywalks and paraded the pieces of bone on his neck.

But those days are long gone. For all his strength, the old man broke easy. Nothing was the same for him without her.

They say he's gone mad, that he was poisoned by grief. I look at him closely, but can tell nothing from his milky eyes. All they do is reflect the fire.

"The Night of the Clean Hands is a bad bargain." He croaks to the crowd. "Will you sell yourself so cheap? Is one night of happiness all you need? Why take so little when the princess can offer you her love for a lifetime?"

They all cheer for him. The crowd hangs on his every word.

"She knew every single one of us, gave us the chance to share in her bed. We all took comfort that she was here and we were not alone. That girl had nothing but love to give."

He wipes the sweat off his bald head, "You had it good. Our girl was all you ever needed, everything you ever wanted. She gave you the means to forget everything that was real and the chance to share in her fame. But when the princess needed you the most, when death came to claim her, you were not there by her side. She died alone. Mother, forgive us!"

The preacher pulls out his stump. An outgrowth of scar tissue covers the nib of the amputation. The crowd goes quiet. "Have you atoned? Begged her for forgiveness? I have a ghost hand, here. That was my sacrifice. What was yours?

"She is lost to us now. Our girl is on the other side. An ocean of darkness spreads between the world of the living and the land of the dead. But death doesn't have to be the end of it. Our love for her is stronger than the grave. We can still show the princess the way home.

"Look at what I have found: a perfect little thing, just like her. Another Venus who was made to hang."

A girl slinks from the back of the room. She comes out of nowhere. The crowd kneels as she approaches. She moves on her tiptoes, her movements slow and awkward, body contorted like a broken marionette. She falls on her knees in front of the fire. Her hands have been lopped off. The wounds still look wet and fresh. The skin's gnarled at the edges. A pair of rubber hose tourniquets are clamped to her stumps to minimize the bleeding.

She's freshly tattooed. Her body's covered with bandages. Red specks are still wet on the gauze. It's hard to recognize her behind the tattoos and the wig of black pearls. The girl, it's Shih, the oldest of the Kwong sisters.

Hannibal strokes at her cheeks, gently. She smiles at him, cracking open her red lips. Blood spills from the side of her mouth.

The monks remove the gauze off Shih's body, peeling it back like old skin. They reveal her tattoos. Twisted vines, black thorns and rosebuds crown her nipples. She looks perfect.

Hannibal looms over her. He slips a rope over her head and tightens the noose.

"Can you hear it? A low rumble that comes from underground," he smiles, "There's something down there. It's moving. The thing roils.

"The Red Light Princess is not at rest in the grave, my brothers. She's suffering and desperate. Death is a lonely place.

"But I've got news for you. She's broken out and is tunneling through Hell's core, moving between worlds. All she wants is to get back home."

The old man's voice lowers. His eyeballs fill with water.

"It is dark down there. The princess is lost. She needs our help, and I have found a way to guide her back to us."

He places a blank, porcelain mask over Shih's face. "This Venus will hang, and her beauty will shine like a flare. Each one of these girls who dies will cross over to the other side, their bodies hanging like stars from Hell's black sky. They are beacons to show the princess the way out from the land of the dead and back to the world of the living.

"The princess tunnels through the black rock. It won't be long now. She will be done with her digging before dawn. Our princess comes back to us tonight. And when she does, that girl is owed her revenge."

His milky eyes turn on me. I can feel their deadpan stare. He comes from behind the fire, reaches out, and grabs my shoulder. The old man draws me in. Hannibal's breath smokes hot on my face.

"But we must be careful," the preacher says. "This place is a wilderness, man-eaters roam everywhere."

I light up a cigarette, trying to look cool and in control. The smoke curdles my stomach.

The preacher draws back my hood, "You know this better than most, little cub."

His one good hand looks exaggerated, ridged and bound into a fist. He punches me in the gut. I slouch over, swallowing back a gag.

The old man picks me up by my collar and presses his face against mine. A wet snort splashes on my cheek. He pulls back his head, cocking his neck like a trigger, and slams his forehead against the bridge of my nose.

I fall back on the pavement. My head pounds. I try to cough but only manage to gurgle a spray of blood out of my mouth. My sight's blurred. The preacher's face turns fuzzy, a reception I just can't catch. My eyes go out of focus.

He's losing definition and melting into the background.

I take in mouthfuls of air, desperate for oxygen, choking on the blood. Every breath is labored. I feel like I am shutting down. It's getting colder. Everything seems distant. The ground sinks underneath me.

Sweats spills from the preacher's bald head. It splashes on me and gets in my eyes. The taste of his salt is on my tongue.

Hannibal gives me a solid kick to the side of my head, and the pain knocks me out.

Chapter Ten
Hanging Venus

I wake up and turn on my belly to cough out the blood. My head's pounding. Cold sweat's got me drenched under my pits.

There's blood all over my sweatshirt. It has soaked right through my hoodie. The stuff is sticky and cold on my skin.

My eyes dart around the room. There is a rope wrapped around the base of a column. The rope is stretched tight, but it moves from side to side with the weight of the load it's carrying. I pluck on it like a one string guitar.

I grip the width of the rope and follow it to a window in the back. The glass has been smashed. Blood marks splatter on the frames. I swallow hard before I look over the edge.

Shih's body hangs over the streets. The girl, her pose— they're all perfect. She looks just like her.

A large crowd has already gathered to watch her from every rooftop and skywalk around the block. It's much bigger than the one that gathered for her sister. The No Go Zone roars with noise out there.

My implants are sensitive. They're picking up every bit of resonance from the ghettos. They vibrate through me. It's overwhelming. I can hardly breathe.

Buzzards start to fly in. They've got their spotlights on her. The drones congregate around the body, buzzing around it and puffing smoke. Their cams relay the live footage onto the screens.

One of the buzzards spots me. The drone shoots up to the window, its lens aiming straight at me. Red lights flicker around the eye of the camera

The buzzard stares me down. Its spotlights flash on me.

It starts uploading the feed off its camera. My face flashes and dissolves on the massive screens. The close-ups zoom in on the blood on my clothes, the gun in my holster, and the girl hanging from the rope.

I look back at the drone and shake my head, trying to reason with the machine, "I'm a 25. You got the wrong idea here. This dead girl is not on me."

The drone is not buying it. We stare each other down. The thing eyes me suspiciously.

Two more buzzards fly up to the drone's flanks. Their motors rev. Smoke blows from their exhausts. They blast off their boosters and shoot straight at me.

I back away from the window and run.

I look over my shoulder, and sure enough they're closing in. The buzzards shriek. They speed through the hallway, their rotor blades tilted, coming straight at me.

I run into the stairwell and jump the railing. My body shoots down the shaft, making a dive for the lobby.

The drones close in in me. They lock in on my body heat. I feel their spotlights on the back of my neck. They ride tight on my tail, making this spiraling kamikaze drop on me.

I turn back and fire my snubby at them, blasting a couple of rounds. I make a direct hit on one of the buzzard's fuselages. It explodes over my head and takes another down with it. The rotor blades swoop down the stairwell, and shrapnel skids all around me.

The last of the drones breaks through the wreck and tackles me. It knocks my wind out, and we both crash into the lobby.

We roll around on the ground. The drone tries to pin me. Its beak bites down on my shoulder. I scream and pop two bullets into its head.

We smash against the wall. The buzzard's heavy and weighing over my chest. Its landing skids dig into my sides.

I manage to push it off and get back on my feet. The drone's head squirms on the ground. I roll it around under my talons and crush the camera's lens.

It smells like some of my hair got burned off in the wreck. It's my rattail. The ends got singed a bit.

I should be in more pain. A piece of shrapnel's dug deep into my arm. I've got a cut straight across my belly. Warm blood drips from my mouth. But I'm not feeling much. The morpho replica masks everything. My jaw is the only thing that is sort of sore. I pop my mandible to ease the pressure.

The doors to the lobby crash open, and a squad of 25's storm inside.

The men fan out and surround me. They got me clocked with the night scopes on their sidearms. A pair of drones back them up. The buzzards aim their spotlights right at me.

I catch her off the corner of my eye. Mercury's earrings are smashed disco balls. Her exoskeleton is painted in yellow and black hazard stripes.

She slides her hand over a foot soldier's flat Kevlar belly and squeezes through the firing line, "Step aside, boys."

Mercury walks up to me shaking her head. She pulls me closer by my rattail. Her lips buzz at my ears. "Well, what do you know?"

Chapter Eleven
Mercury

A convoy pulls up on the curb. The rickshaws' engines purr. Their taillights are broken, hazards blinking one-eyed.

Mercury and I climb into a rickshaw and pull into traffic. The rest of the convoy beats their horns and burns rubber behind us.

Mercury's covered a black eye under a cake of foundation. Her knuckles are scuffed. Fresh stitches needle the back of her neck. Mercury's a natural brawler. She likes to get her hands dirty. This is why I like her. The girl is something familiar to me.

"You don't look so good, handsome," she says.

"I'm just having one of those days. I've been thrown off an elevator. An albino monster chewed on my leg like a milk bone. My nose got broken. And I crash-landed wrestling with one of your fucking buzzards."

"I've got to hand it to you." Mercury flashes me her jade smile." You sure know how to take a beating."

"You are not worried about me are you?"

"Sorry, Kai, I must've given you the wrong impression. I don't like you."

"Are you sure about that?"

"That was one night, all vodka and hits of amphetamine replica. It could have been anybody."

I lick at one of the scrapes running up my forearm, nurs-

ing the wound, "You have to do something about those buzzards. They almost killed me. Those bastards are on a hair
trigger."

"They found you covered in blood over a hanging dead
girl. Who can blame them? We are all on edge tonight. Dead
Girls are dropping like flies."

Our convoy's stuck in traffic. The streets are up to their
fill. Tourists lug around shopping bags and souvenir T-shirts.
They take pictures of the skywalks, slowing everything down.

I light up two smokes. Mercury takes one, and I keep the
other clenched between my teeth. "This isn't over. There's
another girl out there, and she's going to hang."

"So go ahead, spill it. Tell me something I don't know
about these dead girls?"

"There's three of them. They're called the Kwong sisters.
The girls were Red Light Princess Impersonators—good ones.
They looked just like her."

"The preacher and his monks are hanging these girls. It's
a ritual or something. The old man's gone crazy. He thinks it
will bring his girl back to life."

"It won't."

"You tell him that…"

She swirls the cigarette in her mouth and munches on
the filter, "Why didn't you take Hannibal down?"

"He's a strong bastard. He took me out with a head-butt.
I lost him."

Mercury punches my throat, closing the windpipe. I
have to be careful with her. A punch from her exoskeleton
can hit at about two thousand pounds of pressure.

"Now you're gonna find him." She pulls me up by my
hair. "A bag of old bones with just one hand… Did I send the
wrong man?"

I try to scrape my voice, channel my brother, sound no-nonsense and manly. But there is something off. It's coming out wrong. I sound like a scared kid. "Listen to me. All I need is time. Give me a couple of hours. I'll make things right between us."

"These Kwong sisters are getting a real following. They're getting the crowds all worked up. Protests have already exploded in three districts. The people are demanding justice. This place we live in… It holds together on a thread. The Night of the Clean Hands is the knot. Untie it and everything falls to pieces. I told you these dead girls can get dangerous."

"I know it…"

"The countdown's getting close to nightfall. I want the preacher before sundown. Taking down Hannibal has its benefits. He's a legend. You know what happens to the man who kills a legend, handsome? He becomes one himself."

I meet her eyes, but she looks unmoved. "I'll find him for you."

"One man dies so the rest of us don't have to. That's the way it's always been. The Night of the Clean Hands demands sacrifice. Next time we meet, you will have the preacher with you. I will take no more excuses. I will get my man by sundown. All I need's a body. If you don't bring me the one I want, yours will have to do."

"I'm on it." I step out of the rickshaw.

Mercury parts the aluminum privacy beads, her inky eye on me, "Be careful, Kai. You know how these sacrifices go better than most. Isn't that how your brother went down? His body torn apart by Mecha Beasts?"

My face is expressionless: a thing of stone. I'm mastering this moment. She won't see anything but what I show her.

"That's right. They picked him clean and then munched

on the bones. We never got back a single piece."

Chapter Twelve
Otto the Shock Bear

I land on a window ledge and sit down for a breather and a smoke. The public screens show a slow-mo, zoomed in replay of the last fight. 'Otto the Shock Bear vs. Gorilla-xe' scrolls down in a bloody font.

It's the semifinals. The Mecha Beast Wars are getting close to the big fight of the night. Everybody's eyes turn on the screens. They are impossible to ignore. There's nothing like death seen through a big badass jumbotron.

The bear is huge. His fur is spiked up and bleached an arctic white. The metallic armature round his back is ridged with a barbed spine.

Gorilla-xe goes at the bear with its axe heads. The ape howls, desperate to get a hit. But Otto moves too quickly, dodging and swerving away from the blades.

The ape lands a couple of hits, but they get deflected off the bear's armor.

Otto gets up on his back legs and roars. Red and black wires are coiled round his iron muzzle. He gets all the attention from the crowd. And the beast loves it, roaring back at them.

His hair is bleached like a polar bear, but thick black roots show underneath. He has it styled in spikes and looks badass. My hair's made up just like his.

The bear lunges and swipes his claws at the ape. He is

nothing if not precise. An eyeball rolls out on the ring.

The gorilla starts screaming. It sounds pitiful and human. Otto takes his chance and jumps on the other animal's back. He bites into the ape's neck until its body starts convulsing with the electric current and the spine breaks.

Johnnie Manila's teeth are huge on the screen. His under bite makes them look gritted, filed and stuck out like a barracuda. "Kill Move! No quarter given, ladies and gentlemen. Otto the Shock Bear is going on six straight wins tonight. Look at him go. This big boy is on a roll!"

The gorilla's body is charred and smoking. Otto looms over it. He digs into the ape's belly, scrounging for the choice organs. His iron muzzle is wet with blood. The thing sparks and smokes when it touches wet flesh.

Otto is such a media whore. He stands on his hind legs, roaring, playing it up for the crowd.

They lap it up and cheer for him. The fans hoot and wave his black and white banners. A round of stray bullets goes off. Girls lose their tops and scream out his name.

"The girls love the Shock Bear," Johnnie Manila cackles into the camera.

We build up celebrities easily here. They tower above us on the public screens: huge and terrifying and out of our reach.

Hannibal is still out there. I need to find him or it's going to be me in that ring getting fried and eaten before dawn.

I look up at the sky, but the moon is lost in the smog. The night's just racing by, and my time is running out. And there is still one more sister left to drop.

I jump off the ledge and keep on moving.

I go through the central gate to the Burned Market and blend in with the crowd of shoppers. My hood is on. Head is slumped. Hands are in my pockets. I take an easy pace, keeping my movements slight, making sure that nothing about me stands out.

I try to blend: look casual. There's nothing special about me. I'm just a wanderer on the streets, another urban ranger in this wayfarer scene.

There's no talent in hiding. Go about your business. Nobody is really paying attention.

I move past a row of rickety stands. They're lined with beads and plastic dividers. I stop by one of the stands and pick up a dehydrated seahorse. It looks phony in its cellophane packaging. The thing is brittle and doesn't weigh a thing. It has the feel of a cheap toy that is about to come apart in my hands. I toss it back into the pile.

The Burned Market is the closest thing to a natural geological formation in the No Go Zone. This entire block was hit by a gas pipeline explosion. The blast tunneled through every single one of the buildings. It hollowed them out, collapsing entire floors and generating a new, unclaimed space. The urban terrain shifted; environment and architecture melted together.

After decontamination it was settled by a rush of entrepreneurial squatters. They occupied the remains, renovated and rebuilt, forming the largest unlicensed market in the greater metropolitan area.

The walls are still scorched and punctured by large, crooked openings that connect the buildings into one continuous structure.

I make a turn at the shops on the corner. An old woman scoops a handful of dates from a wicker basket and offers me a good deal. I spot migrants huddling in the dark corners slow-roasting each other's fingerprints with cigarettes. Girls glide across the market draped in well pressed burqas, their little feet concealed by the flow of the fabric.

I step on a frothy mixture of soap and blood pooled on the ground. There are chickens and wild fowl stuffed into mesh-wire crates all around me. Their chests are puffed, beaks wet with mucus. They scramble, pecking at each other for space.

Tsang Man Fai's kebob stand is at the rear of the market, near the back lot for the fortune tellers and clowns. He's got his sunglasses on and is searing a batch of mystery meat on the grill. A hundred kids run barefoot, screaming around him. They're all filthy, noses crusted, eyes patched over, and covered in piercings. The kids huddle together sharing puffs of replica residue from a yellowed light bulb. They follow me as I step up to the stand.

I rattle my knuckles on the aluminum counter, "What do you got cooking in there?"

"I can't tell you that." Tsang Man Fai wipes his hands on his butcher's apron. "I'd ruin half the fun for you."

"Where do you find your meat?" I ask.

"My babies get it for me. They're good at scavenging for fresh kill." His smile is all pink jade teeth and paper-thin wrinkles. "These kids are crafty. Nobody sees them coming."

"I bet…" I eye the little bastards suspiciously.

The kebob stand is a front. Tsang Man Fai runs a private intelligence outfit. He takes in every stray kid and orphan that's out there looking for cash to eat, drink, or get high. The guy sends them out into the No Go Zone as his eyes and ears to spy and collect valuable information for his clients.

Tsang Man Fai is expensive but worth it. He brings

wayward husbands kicking and screaming back home to their wives, finds stalkers their long lost loves again. He sells intelligence briefings to the triads and gangs.

They say he has been around the world—grew up barefoot and sharp as a knife, teaching himself to read and hustle. He spent his life in a global slum pilgrimage. The man's seen it all. He ran guns to the warring gangs in the dire parts of Cité Soleil, rioted with the black blocs in central Berlin, and ran the heroin trade in the squatter encampments of the Old City of Lahore. The No Go Zone is the last place left open to him.

He lowers the heat on the grill. "What are you doing out in the open? I thought your kind was good at skulking around in the dark."

"I hate the market. The fucking smell is unbearable. This place is all sweat, shit and animal fear."

"Mind your tongue. Not in front of the kids."

I pull out my snubby and borrow my brother's voice again. "Don't play this daddy dearest game with me. I'm a 25."

His kids' eyes pause on me. They whisper to each other, using a secret language, something they've invented to connect with themselves alone. The kids move closer to me, drawing out knives.

I put away my snubby. My voice is my own again, weak and childish. "They're jumpy fuckers."

A patch of his white curls dangles over his shades. "It's that amphetamine replica. Makes them all riled."

I pick up a piece of the mystery meat from the grill and pop it in my mouth. It's plain and rubbery. I have no idea what's swirling around my tongue. The meat turns to taffy as I chew.

"I need to find the preacher." I flick my rattail over my shoulder.

"Why would you want to do a thing like that? That old man is insane. You don't want those monks of his coming after you to tear at your limbs and split you to pieces."

"You know how it goes. I want your eyes. "

"These eyes?" Tsang Man Fai takes off his shades. His eye sockets are scorched with black scar tissue, the holes empty. The caverns seem to go for miles into his skull.

"No. The eyes you own."

"Nobody will tail the preacher, Kai. None of my babies are dumb enough to do it. They have enough sense not to poke at a mad bear."

"Hannibal's been hanging girls from the skywalks. He's got another one ready to drop. This has to stop. I can't bear to see another one go down. They look just like the princess."

He shuts off the stove and skewers the meat on a stick. "Everybody grieves in his own way. Let that old buzzard go on his rampage."

"The preacher and I have something between us."

"Don't say I didn't warn you," he sighs, and his voice lowers, "The old man likes to visit the princess's shrine on the anniversary of her death. He brings her a bouquet every year. Go to the Red Lake right on kilometer zero. The old man you seek is by the waters now."

Chapter Thirteen
Kilometer Zero

I slide down the back of a building and hit street level. My eyes have to adjust to the darkness.

I stay off the main roads and keep to a network of back alleys bordering the western separation barrier. Crinkled, yellowing sunscreen models smile down at me from the outdated billboards. The magnetic energy from the city outside seeps through the walls and buzzes at my implants. I can't help but wonder what is out there.

Time's running out on me. I pick up my pace and walk past a few more blocks. The fluorescent lights on the sidewalk flicker on and off. I follow a chain link fence that runs to the end of a backstreet. I climb over it and jump to the park on the other side.

They call this place the Commons. It's a sprawling concrete courtyard at the center of the No Go Zone: a free transit area that's not under the protection of any triad or clan. Every road in the slums leads back to this place. Everything is measured from where I stand. I'm at kilometer zero.

I take a walk by the old telephone booths. The payphones have been ripped out and tossed. Every booth is hollow and padded with cushions. They've been given a new use. The compartments were refurbished as privacy booths for a quick toke or a fuck. Every one of them is busy.

I trek to the other side of the park. My talons are slippery.

They sink into the mud. The soles are caked in it. They feel heavy and slow me down.

There's a large crowd gathered along the Red Lake. Hundreds of men and women hold up candles, burn incense and pray. Above, thousands more peek from their windows. Gawkers, dancers and curiosity seekers are packed against the railings of the upper skywalks.

The lake used to be a community pool. They say the princess used to come here and skinny dip by the moonlight. The night she was killed, her fanboys and believers came here to pray, sacrifice, and toss offerings into the water. The pool was red with blood that night, swimming with body parts.

A group of women by the shallow end light incense and candles. Their naked bodies are painted a hot dahlia red. The believers are a mix of old and young bodies, breasts of every shape, size and texture. Black, wiry muffs spike from between their legs.

The women kneel at the pool's edge, tossing in an offering of legs, arms and minced meat. This old girl with white hair down to her back and track marks up her arms bites down on her own fingers, chewing them off one by one, spitting the remains back into the fountain.

She shows the crowd her mangled hand, and they start cheering. The old gal smiles. She's caught their attention. They're in her hands. Her chest puffs up. She soaks it in—the wonder of it. All eyes are on her. For this small moment, the world is hers.

The water is a thick jelly. It's black with flies. Body parts bob in the stew.

The stench of the decomposing meat and the incense rolls into a toxic cloud. It makes me sick. I let my head swing between my legs.

My breath grows short. I'm hit with a cold wave. The insides of my skull prickle. I feel the shakes coming back with a vengeance.

I slump to the ground, hold my knees against my chest and puke out an increase of bile.

I'm getting stepped on. Trampled. But I don't move an inch. I don't want to get up. It feels comfortable here on the ground. Natural. Right for me.

A rat scurries around nearby. It is red-eyed and spotted. The animal comes closer. It sniffs at my talons and runs off.

I watch the rat maneuver through the crowd. It's weaving in a zigzag, unstoppable, finding a way out of the maze. The rat works with the environment and adapts to the shifts in the terrain.

I'm down at the animal's level, becoming something more recognizable, a kindred species sharing the same low space. My perspective changes. I see with new vermin eyes. I sense different paths that weren't clear before: alternative spatial paradigms that only rats are aware of. We're kindred species, bottom feeders sharing the same hunting ground.

My body shifts inward and contracts. The ends of my coat drag behind me like a tail. I scurry on the roof, a quadruped keeping to the fringes. My teeth are out and gritted.

A child clings to his mother's leg and screams. She holds him close and recoils from me. The transformation is complete.

I scuttle over to the nearest dumpster and hide below its wet underbelly. There's an air-conditioning set pissing from a couple of floors up. I lap up the water running on the pavement.

My eyes veer across the crowd. I spot Hannibal kneeling at the edge of the Red Lake. He stands out, a large and lumbering target. His bald head shines like a tailgate.

The preacher cradles a bouquet of severed arms wrapped in newspaper and coos into the black water.

The crowd gets thicker the closer I get to him. I weave through the mess of bodies, using my elbows to push through, inching nearer. I want to catch him off guard: jump him when he least expects it. He can't see me coming.

The preacher turns his head back. His milky eyes bulge. I feel them scanning the park, lingering in my direction. Hannibal waves his stump at me.

I go at him and jump on his back. The preacher shuffles me off like I don't weigh a thing. I hit the ground on my back.

Hannibal picks me up by the neck, my talons scraping on the pavement, and tosses me into the pool.

I gurgle on the black muck. The water sticks to my body like oil. It seeps into my throat with the aftertaste of blood and rot.

I come out of the water and crawl back to the pavement. The bite on my leg throbs. Every bruise feels tender and alive. I roll myself over, pull out a fistful of wet cigarettes from my pocket, and mesh them into a ball.

I get back on my feet and scan the park for the preacher. Hannibal climbs up a fire escape. He scrambles his way to the roofs. I wring the water out from rattail and run after him.

A magnetic pulse blasts from my launchers. The wave scatters through the atmosphere. It measures the distance between the buildings, gives me a sense of the obstacles and traffic conditions: a spatial schematic of the jump to the next roof.

I dive off and barely make it to the other side. My body half hangs from the edge of the building. I pull myself over and get back on my feet.

I work a light sweat, trotting past the exhaust vents on the roof. My rattail beats behind me. The obstacles keep me sharp. I sidestep a couple of firework stands, break through a prayer circle of nuns with my elbows.

I'm after him, moving quickly and gaining ground. My needs are basic: pouncing on my catch and having my fill. The hunt keeps me going. It's all about the chase. I have to forget everything else, zero in and track the preacher down.

The thrill of the chase brings out something primal in me. My hairs stand up. I don't want to look back. All there is lays in front of me. I'm single-minded; move forward, keep going, one foot in front of the other.

Hannibal free jumps bareback. He's clean. The preacher's got nothing on him. No magnetic perception implants, augmentations, hydraulic-stilts or gliders. The old man flies on a prayer. That fucker is fearless.

He dives into a spider web of skywalks ten stories down. I jump right after him.

My heart beats against my ribcage. I swoop down, coming up behind him.

Electric prickles spark at my nerve endings. Senses heightened, I can smell the trail of his sweat in the air, almost taste the salt off his skin. My mouth sops with saliva. Hunger has set in.

I reach out and catch his tunic. Luck is with me. He's in my grip.

Hannibal turns around and bashes his head against mine. I jerk back but manage to keep my hold on his tunic. We drop fast and whirl out of control.

We crash-land on a skywalk and roll around on the deck. I kick-start my crampons and stab the spikes into his leg, slicing deep into the muscle.

The preacher falls back. A flap of meat hangs from his calf. He grips at the sliver and tears it off.

Hannibal tosses the piece of meat over the rails, "You think you're on the prowl, little cub? But you got it all wrong. I'm not your dinner. You have it the other way around. Beat it and run back to your pack mama's side. We will have our moment, you and I."

I'm supposed to be the one on the chase here, tracking down my catch. But it doesn't feel like it. We're finally face-to-face, and all I can do is freeze. A deer in the headlights, hypnotized by the lights. I suddenly realize he's right. I'm not the hunter here at all.

"We need to talk," I pull back my hood.

"You don't look like a man-eater." His milky eyes look me up and down. "But you've sure tasted the flesh."

"Come with me." I offer him my hand. "You don't know what's coming your way."

He smiles, "What kind of fool gives his last hand over? I should have put you down the moment I laid eyes on you."

I'm close enough to smell his breath. The old man's pickled in rum. The smell is dizzying.

"We don't have much time. Stop running from me."

"Who says I'm running?" He shakes his head and smiles. "I can't play this game with you, little cub. I'm late."

"You're a religious man. You can't hang that boy. Not tonight."

"Those sisters were perfect little things. They looked just like her. But it was the boy who was something special. He was the princess born again in his wigs and makeup. I had to save him for last. When that beauty hangs, he'll light up like a comet in the skies of Hell. The boy will die just like her and work his magic. He will show her the way and get this whole thing started. My girl's coming home."

We nod and there's a connection: a strange acknowledgement that we each know the other's number. We don't say a word, but share the moment. The Red Light Princess has gotten into our heads. Men like us dropped from the roofs by the hundreds the night she died.

We both know the madness of devotion.

Hannibal flings himself off the skywalk. The preacher's body curls into a ball, going down in a dunk. He crashes against a fire escape and dangles from the rails.

I run over to the edge and look down at the height of the fall. My rattail beats with the wind.

Chapter Fourteen
The Parade

I stumble around in the crowd, single-minded, fighting for space with the other spectators, using my elbows to crack through the solid block of bodies.

They are all out in mass to watch the parades go by the skywalks. Slum tourists take pictures. Kids climb up the utility poles and wave their banners. On the higher floors, gawkers and curiosity seekers look down from the windows.

The parades spill from every rooftop on the block: Waves of bodies and noise, incoming from every direction. The throng howls. They are whipped up, dancing. Everybody drinks on the go, pulling smoke from a rolling, wheeled hookah.

A troupe of disk jockeys carries speakers strapped to their backs. They blast off rivaling beats, composing improvised streams. Free jumpers in glow-in-the-dark skeleton suits spin to their music.

You never know when the parades are coming. They just go off in the different sectors of the No Go Zone. All it takes is a spark: one man to take to the streets with a drink and a beat, and then another to join to him. It's an organic outburst of people, spillover from the celebrations out there, the old tradition of the riot. A rolling, breathing, meat eating, heavy drinking party. They get bigger and bigger, picking up strays and drunks as the night goes on.

Fireworks go off above me. A pyrotechnic monster spreads its wings in the sky. The crowds cheer.

My implants buzz. Something feels off. I don't want to look over my shoulder, but I do it anyway. Morien and Sonya come up behind me. Their dog sniffs the air, catching my scent.

It starts barking when it spots me. My brother's head turns towards me. He springs his blades out and tries to break through the crowd. But it's thick as jelly out here. And that slows him down.

I try to find a way out but the crowd is only growing. It never stops. More people come in. Everybody wants their fair share of the party, to be a part of the spectacle.

Space is getting tight. The air is tacky. I take solid bites of air.

I drop on my hands and knees to stay out of sight, back on bottom feeder level. I stumble around, going in between legs, sifting through the spectators, and pushing my way out of the crowd.

Morien catches up with me. Those insectoid scythes of his hack at me. I roll on the ground, dodging the scythes and scrambling to get away. He's got me all cut up. I'm bleeding. But he hasn't gotten a deep puncture wound in yet. I know his game. He wants to drive those puppies through my body and pin me to the ground.

My holster gets cut off me in the scuffle. Both guns roll around on the ground. I reach out for my jet-gun, but it gets smashed before I can reach it. The snubby gets lost in the mess of bodies.

I manage to give him the slip and mix with dancers on the parade. Girls wearing animal masks dance all around me. Foxes, google-eyed pandas, and kittens in black vinyl minis.

They're getting closer and closer to the edge of the skywalk. More than one of them goes over.

Two girls grind and paw at each other, lifting each other's skirts over their hips. They're dressed as a raccoon and a snake with sequined, lozenge-shaped scales. The girls raise their masks, kiss, pulling at their tongues with their teeth.

I snatch the raccoon mask off one of them and put it on myself, blending with the other dancers. My head bops, picking up the beat. I take a drag from one of the tentacles of the wheeled hookah. The smoke blows out my nostrils. It's a cheap ganja replica, but it does the job. I feel my muscles just melt away. They slip off the bone.

I grab this strange girl's hand and take her deeper into the crowd. We twirl around. Her face is a blur. She's nothing but streaks of black and gold, her mouth moving like an optical reverb.

I don't dare let go of her. We have to keep on moving. I can never stop. If I stop there's no helping it. I'm good as dead.

Sometimes I feel tired. I would like to let them catch up with me. End this once and for all. Get what I got coming. But who am I kidding? I'm too scared of paying back what I owe.

The beat picks up on the speakers. It races into an aggressive, amped pace. The procession starts getting fevered. The dancer's movements are faster, less coordinated, slightly out of control.

A couple of boys start it in the back, and others join in. The crowd starts pushing and slamming against each other. They get more intense, using their elbows and swinging bottles. The procession piles up into a violent mosh.

A fight breaks out in front of me. I crouch down to avoid getting hit in the scuffle. One of the women bounces on her heels, holding a brick in her hand. The other is wearing pigtails and a razor-blade bracelet twisted up her arm.

Morien pushes through the dancers. He stops any man he can grab and pulls off his mask. His Doberman sniffs out the rest.

Sonya has this kid choked up in a neck hold. He's shirt-less, wearing a fresh-cut crocodile head over his shoulders. She takes the carcass off his face and then tosses it over the rails. Bloods runs down his ribs and pools at the belly button.

I join in the violence, elbowing at random. I feel full of purpose, single-minded. An electric prickle runs from my implants to the marrow in the bones. I carve a path out of the mess of bodies.

My implants start buzzing again. They pound, hot and urgent. I feel it in my gut. Every magnetic instinct tells me to get down and duck. I hit the floor just as his scythes slice over my head.

Morien swipes his blades at me. Angry lines crawl at the sides of his mouth. He goes at me again, full strength. I bring out my talons and parry them away with a kick.

I climb over the railing and jump off the skywalk. My body rolls on the rooftop below. I skid and my talons scratch-mark the ground. Sparks burn at my feet. My crampons are hot with the friction. A couple of spikes come loose like teeth. The two front points get all twisted.

Morien hasn't given up the chase. He lands behind me. I go as fast as I can. But I can't outrun him. His third gen modifications got me beat. He sprints closer like a wild animal, mouth unhinged, scythes out, four-legged on the ground.

His body is half-covered in the dark, purring like some cornered animal. He springs off his back legs and comes straight at me.

We roll around, bucking and flipping over. He goes at

me with his fists, bashing my eye socket, cheek, and bursting my lip open. Blood gushes on my face. My head recoils and pounds on the ground.

His thumbs are on the black circles under my eyes. Breath puffs into my mouth. I try to push him off me, but he won't budge. Morien's scythes spring out and drive through the meat of my shoulder, pinning me to the ground.

I scream. The edges of the scythes are serrated. They cut me up inside as he twists the blade.

I kick start my talons and cut into his thigh. The skin just peels back. A pair of hydraulic pistons are implanted inside. They hyperextend as he works the muscle.

I manage to get him off me and run.

There's a giant, warped balloon of the Red Light Princess dangling from the backside of a building across the street. Her stumps flap with the wind. The balloon moves lazily, looking stoned out of its mind. But I don't know if this is real. Can't trust what I see. All my senses are scrambled. I run to the edge of the roof and dive over to her.

I land on the balloon's leg and slip down the calf. Part of the princess's dress dislodges and tumbles to the ground. She swings from side-to-side. I can barely hold on. My grip is giving in.

I look up. My brother is still on me. Morien holds on to a groove on the princess's belly. He slices his blades into her womb and pops the balloon. Helium sprays out and her skin begins to deflate. The balloon tumbles to the ground, bringing me down with it.

I spin around in the air, close my eyes, cover my face with my elbows, and brace myself for the landing.

My body hits the nets and lands on a pile of scrap metal, motherboards, cracked television screens and a couple of dead buzzard drones. I climb down from the heap and pull out the pieces of broken microchips stuck to the back of my leg.

The balloon collapses in slow-mo as the helium empties into the atmosphere. Its wrinkled stumps still move, reaching out to the sky.

My implants start buzzing. There's movement all around me. I turn my head from side to side.

I got the dog spotted at my left, Sonya coming at me from the rear, my brother crawling from under the balloon. They keep on their bellies, hands and feet gripped on the web.

The currents beat against me. A draft of wind slices at my cheeks. A burst of microclimate whirls through the alleyways, blowing trash off the ground in an upsurge.

I kick start my talons, cut a hole through the net, and jump through it.

Chapter Fifteen
Rats

I shook off the family a couple of blocks back. The hole on my shoulder throbs. Every bruise feels tender and alive. It's just a flesh wound, but it hurts badly. The blade went through the side of my delt and out the rear.

Sweat pours down my back. Every bone in my body is sore. The hole on my shoulder feels like it's chewing on itself.

I break through a window on the eighth floor and hop inside the building. It leads into a corridor. The carpet's scratched and worn down to the bare cement base. Every doorway is padlocked, gated behind barbed-wire screens. Hazard symbols warning against the threat of zoonotic infection plaster the walls.

An awful stench wafts through the air. The funk is ripe and has just turned to a sugary rot. It gets worse the deeper I go.

I fall on my knees and throw up a wad of green bile. My stomach's running on nothing but replica and that one beer I had at the brothels. I'm sweating cold and am itching for a hit of morpho.

With each step I send rats off in a scatter. The ground turns shifty, moving in ripples of black fur. I kick into a clutch of them to make way to the stairs.

My implants can sense all of them. They burn under my fingers, picking up the movement of every single one of the rats. It's too much information. They screech like static. I'm overloading. There are too many of them.

Rats keep to the fringes, below eye level. I can almost feel the fur on their backs. They rummage in every room. Some go back to their nests inside the walls. Others jump off the stairs and collect in a pile at the base of the building.

This place is ridden with disease. The No Go Zone is the last known source of an outbreak of bubonic plague. Rats spread everywhere. If were are not careful, all human habitation will be restricted to the upper levels where the infestation is still manageable. They will take over everything else.

Something roils under the wave of rats: a body. It's the Red Light Princess. She bobs and gasps, sinking into the moving rats. I hear her screaming beneath her mask. She reaches out for me.

I cover my mouth and step back.

I slap myself to pull it together. Hannibal is still out there. I have to find him and stop him before the last Kwong sister drops. He says he wants the hanging to be perfect. The old man wants to recreate the princess's death for his ritual. There is only one place he can go: the place where the Red Light Princess's body was hung on that night she left this world — the highest point in the skywalks; the Venus Horn.

I land on the skywalk and look over the railing. The southern separation barriers are still miles off. The skywalks above them spiral into a twisted hive that reaches into the sky. The Venus Horn is an observation deck. It juts out from the topmost skywalk in the shape of a sharp, angular spike, crowning the slums.

I have to hurry if I'm going to make it in time. I mix with the crowd of johns up ahead. They're all window-shopping the girls on the portable brothels. The men are packed together. They push and fight to get ahead in line, getting more of a feel of each other than of any of the girls.

The portable brothels have two stories. The top pods are shaped like watchtowers. They're enclosed in transparent glass to showcase the merchandise. The bottom privacy pod is sealed behind an iron curtain. Inside its stocked with a cot, a sink hole and two coin dispensers, one for the camera and the other to activate the ceiling mirror.

One of the whores looks down on me from her tower. She yawns against the glass, fogging it up and drawing hearts on it. Her body's been tattooed with a web of vines, the skin pigmented a dark red.

Another girl has her arm around her. She smiles at me and hides her face with a porcelain mask. The signs above their heads light up, "Vacant."

My head whips from side to side. Every working girl on the skywalk is made up in exactly the same way, bad ink work, masks and cheap pearl wigs.

I cross over to the other side of the deck. The skywalk is packed with vending machines, and makeshift cinder block grills. Something hoofed and spotted roasts on one of the spits. I have to cover my mouth to keep the taste of the animal's fat from seeping down my throat.

A couple of the girls hang out by the cook fire. The whores have their full getups on and still look hot from their beds. They are slick with sweat. The temporary ink work on their legs is starting to run down the curves of their thighs.

I stop to look up at the public screens. Something about the giant images always pulls me in. Those screens, the video replaying all around me, it's all so seductive. I can't help but look.

The screens replay footage of the night's casualties. It's a public service announcement. Shih and Lin lead the coverage. But the bulk of the body count are accidental deaths. It's mostly drunks and teens. Overdoses, suicides, rickshaw collisions, and everybody's favorite: the droppers.

Droppers make the night for many people out there. The crowds love them. The Night of the Clean Hands would never be the same without them. They could be anybody, really. All it takes is one bad step. Any man can trip or stumble and fall down from the skywalks. These videos always go viral. They call them dropper bloopers.

There's even a drinking game. It's not very clever. You cheer and chug whatever you're drinking just as you spot another one go down.

It all feels heightened when I see it on the screens. Deep zooms capture the details of the falling bodies. The whipping hair and wrinkled faces have quality definition. The danger is more pressing. It's hyped and far better than real.

Watching all those bodies fall makes me feel lucky—like I've dodged a big one. Better men than me have stumbled and taken that last drop. It sort of eats at me because I've seen it: how easy it is to go down. Dying's a fucking breeze.

I come to from my television trance and cross over to the next bridge.

Chapter Sixteen
The Hangman's Oasis

The wound on my shoulder throbs. I decide to get a quick drink before going on the Venus Horn.

The Hangman's Oasis is on the other side of district six. It doesn't look like much from the outside. The walls are bare cement blocks. The sign is blackened with grime.

It is a three-story bit of informal construction: a small, fungal building growing on the roof of a high-rise.

I swing the doors open and step inside. The club has been set up to look like an old theater with the stage surrounded by a ring of private boxes.

The dance floor is still going. It is flooded with bodies. Slum tourists haggle with the girls over the price of a dance. Two boys sneak by the orchestra pit exchanging hits of ketamine with their tongues. A lone dancer spins around barefoot. She's on her tiptoes, wearing a black, feathered wing around her breasts as a top.

A cherubim hangs from a noose roped to a spinning disco ball. It holds on to a digital ticker that counts back to dawn. The Night of the Clean Hands always dies slowly.

I cut through the line to the bar and order a shot from the bartender. He slides the glass across the counter. The vodka goes down in one single glug.

I ask around the bar for the preacher, but nobody is in the mood for confidences.

The slots and poker machines are in the back of the main room. I head over to try my luck. The way I see it, gambling is all about waiting out the odds, riding out a streak of bad luck. I've been losing for weeks, years even, so I'm overdue for a win.

I sit down in front of the machine and hit the deal button. The dealer hits me with a jack of diamonds, the ace of hearts and three random spades. I hold on to the spades and discard the others. A flush is coming. I can feel it in my gut.

No such luck though.

I carry around a bucket of tokens and run a lap around the carousels. No machine catches my eye. But I keep looking. There has to be one out there, heated up just right, a tug away from a payout.

I pick a slot machine propped between the doors to the bathrooms and wrap my fist around the length of the lever. A roll of luck's coming my way. I can feel it. There's no doubt. I pull the lever and send the reels spinning. A mermaid, a pair of crossbones and a grinning devil flash on the screen. No symbols align.

This doesn't surprise me. Every time I think a win is coming, the feeling always turns out to be nothing but a dud. My senses are augmented. But they can still get it dead wrong.

Fuck it. I decide to go for broke: break my streak at all costs. I'm going to force this slot machine to pay out, keep on playing until it starts vomiting tokens or I go bust.

I'm at the edge of the stool. My hand's still clamped to the plastic ball at the end of the handle. The machine sucks down everything I have. But I keep going at it, feeding it tokens, losing every time, desperate for a win.

The roll slows down and comes to a stop one more time. Nothing. Not a god damned thing. I bang my head against the screen.

A waitress hovers over me. She offers me a complementary beer. I pop open the bottle and take a swig. It's lukewarm and tastes filthy, but I drain it down just the same.

I hand her back the bottle, and she passes me a note. The message is written on the back of a folded receipt. It reads, "Come on up. Box #25."

I jump down from the stool and toss the empty token bucket over my head. This is all going nowhere anyway. I'm not feeling it. There's no spark. This machine isn't gonna give it up.

The private box is up through the mezzanine, at the end of the hallway, right above the stage. It has a nice setup. A plush, U-shaped sofa fits against the curb of the balcony. There's a poker table propped in the center. The green felt's scratched and peeling at the edges. A rollaway bar is parked in a nook against the wall.

Mercury looks over the balcony, her back turned on me.

I knock on the door frame before going inside, "You wanted to see me?"

She plops down on the sofa and pats her thighs, "Come here. Sit on momma's lap."

I straddle her and nestle nice and snug on her pelvis. She plays with my belt buckle. Her eyes are blasted and crackled with veins. I lean over and suck on her lower lip. She smells of cheap makeup and gunpowder.

Mercury slips her hands inside my pants. Cold fingers grip my cock. She tugs at me and rolls back the foreskin. "You have cold, dead eyes that reveal nothing. I like that..."

I'm eager and fumbling, biting at her earlobe. "Luck's on my side, then."

"You sure about that?" Mercury flashes her jade teeth.

I don't answer her. Mercury's pants roll down. The scratch of her pubic hairs hardens my erection. I pull her shirt over her tits with my teeth. Her breasts slide across my face.

"Did you get me what I want?" she asks, breathless.

"The old man gave me the slip again. But I'm getting close. It's just a matter of time."

She gnashes her teeth, punches my throat and knocks me down from the sofa, "The countdown's getting close to nightfall. Don't tell me you're still empty-handed?"

I cough up a wad of blood and go to the bar to fix myself a drink: vodka neat. "I'll find him."

"All this trouble to bring back to life an old mummy." She says as she fixes herself up. "What is it about dead cunny that makes you men go mad?"

"Death changes everybody in the eyes of the living." I shoot another drink. "We forget who they were once they go into the ground. They all become something beyond our reach: echoes in people's mind, images stuck in the back of their heads. The only reason we long for them is that we can't have them anymore. It's a fool's game."

"You still like that girl, don't you?" Mercury laughs at me.

I shrug my shoulders, "You have to admit that princess had something. She was special. That girl had the vibe of the old divinity celebrity, the new celebrity."

The Red Light Princess used to be an obsession for me. I knew every inch of her body better than the men who paid for her. I'm just another fanboy who can't let go. I keep seeing her ghost everywhere. We're all lost without her.

Mercury gets up from the couch; her exoskeleton is painted with black and yellow hazard stripes. "All I need is a sacrifice for the people, Kai. The crowds want to see someone die at the end of the night. They have been waiting for this moment all year long. They are starving for it. The people like their traditions. They deserve a real show. If you don't bring me the preacher before dawn, I'll feed your body to the Mecha Beasts in the arena. The animals aren't picky. Any piece of meat will do."

Her mouth buzzes at my ear, "How long do you think you'll last in the arena with those monsters? Want to make one last bet with me before you die?"

"That's a gamble..." I mutter.

"Sounds right up your alley. You've always liked to play your luck, hitting every street game, pachinko parlor and arcade in town. I know what you are. You're a natural born gambler, a man that can't help but lose his shirt every time."

"I've had my share of lucky streaks."

"No you haven't. It's all been in your head. You just pretended they were coming, thought you were owed a win."

She's right. I've just assumed that a lucky streak was coming. All this waiting has been for nothing. There's been no payoff. I thought it was incoming, imminent, some natural reaction, a displacement of mass and energy, the final shift that would balance off my losses and make everything right.

Chapter Seventeen
Shark in the Water

Sweating cold bullets here, weak-kneed and holding on to the handlebars of the elevator. The upward pull of the lift's got me dizzy. My body keeps going into these spasms: quick violent fits—a crackle of electricity spreads in the back of my skull. They don't last but a moment, but they're painful and hitting me in waves.

I have to get myself together. Something is wrong. I feel like shit. My body is about to shut down. I need to get sorted. A hit of replica won't do it for me. I'm in the mood for a binge, a morpho blackout. I know the way I like it: dosing heavy on the first round to feel that familiar rush, keeping the buzz going with hourly incremental hits until it's all over. The slums around me go silent, my implants are numbed and I go to black.

Shit, I can feel it running in my bloodstream already— phantom drug tracers.

But I have to keep moving. Look alive to stay alive. There's no telling how this all is going to end. I've gone too far for far too long to stop now. My console's already mapping the closest route to the Venus Horn.

The elevator doors slide open. I take a breath of cold air and stumble onto the roof.

The Pits is a vice bazaar, nothing but gambling parlors, Pachinko imports, nightclubs and dope dens on a mile-long stretch of rooftops.

Neon signs glare back at me. The roofs are lined with rows of bars and coffin-sized video poker booths. They're all cramped together and welded into a metal armature that fixes the stands on the ground. The construction is makeshift at best, a mess of scrap metal paneling and sheets of corrugated steel.

I pull up my hood and head into the crowd. Shoppers and gamblers pack the roofs. Vendors haggle with their customers over bills of foreign currency. Slum tourists haul shopping bags and souvenir T-shirts and take pictures of the natives with their cell phone cams.

They're all part of a booming informal economy: a black hole sidestepping someone else's free markets.

There's a racket on the next roof. A crowd gathers around the bookies to bet on the GMO fights. I cross over to take a look.

Genetically modified organisms are smuggled into the Zone from the city by the bay. We've pirated their tech, cracked sequencing techniques and reclaimed bits and pieces of their precious patents. There're a few bio hack labs out there experimenting with cloned animal testing already. But all I've seen from them is a two-headed kitten and a trash bag full of abortions.

The animals are kept in these large, sealed aquariums. I see neon lobsters wrestle with their claws. Oversized, mutant grasshoppers pound against the glass. Rats, genetically engineered without pain sensation, go at each other savagely, biting off chunks of meat and fur.

I go over to size up the grasshoppers that are up for the next fight. Both of them are monstrous. The insects stand at about a foot on their spindly legs, squealing this horrible chirp. One of them is green, its eyes reptilian and the odds on favorite to win the match.

The other grasshopper is blood red. It clocks its head from side to side, looking straight at me. I tap at the glass. And it taps back. There's a connection here. We got each other's number. My choice is made.

The bookie takes down bets in a booth by the edge of the roof. The booth is covered in a metal armature, and the counter's window is drilled with air holes. Money and goods pass through a drawer that swivels and pops from the base of the frame.

I slip my fingers into the window's air holes, "Put me down for fifty on Red."

The bookie steps up to the glass. Her sun-tipped hair's slicked back. She wears a leather mini with no top. Her breasts bounce openly. The nipples are covered with silver pasties.

"You sure about that?" she asks. "The green grasshopper is a lock. The word is it's a descendant from a champion bloodline. It's been on a winning streak all night."

I roll a couple of bills and slot them through the air holes. "What can I say? There's nothing between us."

"That's fifty on red." The bookie presses the release lever, and the drawer pops out with my ticket. "Hope she brings you luck."

"It's a girl?"

"That's right." She turns away from me and makes the last call for bets over the speakers.

I try to find a good spot to watch the fight. There's an open patch in the back of the crowd right next to this enormous tank. The thing's leaking. It looks filthy. The water is thick with algae. Something big swims inside.

I lean back on the glass, light up another smoke and

enjoy the show.

Both grasshoppers hover off the ground and stare each other down. The aquarium is circled with a ring of electric bug-zappers. A haunting blue light burns through the glass as the match begins.

The green champ's all squeals. It lunges at Red, head-butting her square in the gut. She tries to fend it off. Get away from it. Fly around it. But the insect keeps coming at her, trying to block her way.

She seems overwhelmed and backs into a corner. The champ places its forelegs on the ground and donkey kicks her with its hinds. Red's sent spinning. She bashes against the glass.

The poor girl is on her back, legs flailing. The champ mounts her. It plays up its manliness for the crowd, humping her lewdly, trying to shame her.

I run my hands over my face. My skin is cold. This is over. Red's gone down. She's got the shakes too. Death throes. That was the last of my cash.

But suddenly she pushes the champ off her. She was only playing dead. Red's wings flap out, and she rushes at that filthy green fucker. She stomps her legs on its thorax, pinning it down. Red opens her pincers and chews off one of its wings. She raises it over her head and then goes for the other.

I jump out and hoot. She did it. That's a fifteen to one payout. I feel like I got a streak building here. Wins make more wins happen. It's all about getting a good roll—ball up the right amount of energy and keep the momentum going.

Red's got the crowd's attention. They've gone quiet. She hovers over the former champ's body. Her outstretched mandibles have the effect of looking fanged. She knows how to play it. Red builds up the suspense. When she finally chomps the head off, the crowd goes crazy and cheers her on. They eat it up.

She crosses her back legs and plays a chirpy song over the other grasshopper's carcass. The girl's a perfect diva. She knows how to get the crowd's juices flowing. And they are loving her back.

I fish my pockets for my winning ticket when the water tank at my back starts rocking. It catches me off guard—fucking scares the shit out of me, in fact.

I'm all instinct right now—working at some basic, functional level. My reflexes are on a hair trigger. I turn around and kick start my talons.

But it's only the animal inside the tank. The thing is riled up in there for some reason. The noise of the crowd only makes it worse. It keeps pounding on the glass.

I step up to the tank and try to make out what's in there, but it's too murky to see through. Whatever it is, it's big. I watch it swim in quick, sudden scuds. The tank rocks back and forth as it moves.

It doesn't seem to like me. The closer I get, the angrier the animal becomes. It bashes its head on the glass harder and harder. I tease the fucker, running my fingers on the glass, blowing it cigarette smoke and kisses.

The tank teeters and looks about to turn over. I jump back just as it comes crashing down. A dead body splashes from the tank and rolls on the floor.

It's a girl. Her skin is bloated and turned blue by the water. She's missing both her hands. They've been cut below the wrist. Her eyeballs have melted away.

The Red Light Princess's body is just like I remember it, tattooed with a sprawling arabesque of rosebuds and vines. The tendrils crawl up to her neck and reach into her eye sockets.

Her body squirms on the ground. A gurgle comes up

from her throat. She vomits a spray of algae and tadpoles at my feet.

My cigarette drops from my mouth. I take a couple of steps back and ask to no one in particular, "Do you see that?"

No one answers me. Eyes turn on me from the crowd. But no one wants to look this way. I'm acting crazy. They try to ignore me, pretend I'm not here.

The shakes hit me heavy. My implants heat up. I take in mouthfuls of air, desperate for oxygen.

The Princess's corpse struggles back on her feet. She sobs quietly. There's pain every time she moves. Her legs are stiff, steps clumsy, arms spread out for balance. The princess is rotted. Her body is already falling apart. Pieces of skin slip off in chunks from her bones.

I'm hit by a wave of vertigo. The ground sinks underneath me. My head spins. I try to call out her name, but no sound comes.

She reaches out to me. Her bones are splintered and push out from her stumps like fingers.

I smile wide for her, take her stump in my hand, and kiss the wound. My eyes never leave her empty sockets. I grin, trying to charm her. I wonder if my face is doing what my mind is projecting. Am I getting it all wrong? Can she see right through my seduction? Nobody knew the game better than her.

"I've missed you most of all," I whisper.

Her body stiffens and she steps back slowly. My hand slides off her stump, running a tear down her decomposing skin.

We're locked in a stare that we can't keep. We both pretend it's not happening. But it's inevitable. She turns her head and I look away.

By the time I have the courage to face her, she's already gone, melted into the atmosphere. I shake my head and start running. I have to get the hell out of here before she comes back.

Chapter Eighteen
Men Always Doubt What They Cannot See

I land on the roof and crouch down behind the legs of a water tower. This chase is over. His bald head shines like a tailgate. The old man is in my sights. I've got him now.

Hannibal paces by the edge of the roof, muttering to himself. He's waiting for the passenger pens to arrive and shuttle him to southern arteries in the skywalk system. He's headed to the Horn.

The cranes shriek above us. They haul the passenger pens from building to building, picking up customers. The cages beat against each other. Commuters are stuffed inside, looking out from behind the bars. They look busy, hiding behind newspapers, fiddling with their phones.

A dwarf collects the fares. He crawls on the cages and tosses back change at the passengers. He hangs upside down with a coin dispenser unit belted around his waist.

The preacher pays the little guy his fare. He hops into an empty cage and holds on to the handlebars.

The crane suspends the passenger pens and sweeps them over the street. This is my chance. I gun it, jump off the edge of the roof, and go overboard.

I slice through the air doing spiraling spins. Body twisting like a screw. Core crunched tight. My gnarled talons are out and brandished.

I land on the preacher's pen with a thud. My chest bashes against the iron chassis. I claw at the mesh wire screen with the crampon's spikes. My hands are sweaty and slipping off the bars. A cold pang drips down my spine.

The preacher opens the pen's door and offers me his hand. I reach for it. But he quickly pulls it away.

"Wait a minute… You aren't here for my other hand are you?" Hannibal's voice booms across the nighttime sky. "It's my last one, you know?"

"I didn't cut that thing off."

"You might not have held the knife or sliced through the bone. But you know it. You are guilty just the same." He reaches for me and pulls me inside.

I manage to get back on my feet. It's hard to keep my balance up here. The pen keeps bouncing and jerking from side to side.

Hannibal's milky eyes are on me. I can't help but look away, can't bear to meet his gaze. The whites seem to melt down his face—the slow drip of wax from a candle.

I know what I am better than most. I'm a guilty man with no forgiveness coming, none earned and none deserved.

I force myself to man up to the moment and look him in the eye, "I've come here to warn you. You're in danger."

Hannibal's not listening to me. He's lost in some other moment. His tunic catches a pocket of wind and inflates like a sail.

"Can you feel it?" he asks, "The earth is moving. It's her. She's tunneling her way out from the grave. The Red Light Princess is out there somewhere. She's digging under our feet. One more girl to drop, and she'll find her way home."

"There's nothing down there. This is all in your head."

"You're an unbeliever, little cub. But that's because all you know is the hunt and the wild. You have not seen the things that she has shown me."

"There is no one there." I whisper, "Trust me."

"Men always doubt what they cannot see."

"Your daughter's dead, old man. Her body is on display in the mausoleum."

"That is a rotted carcass!" The preacher pushes me back to the edge of the pen. "My girl is out there: lost. I can hear her, you know. Her screams are loud enough to cross the emptiness between here and the grave."

His voice races. He's got the shakes. There's water in his eyes. He grieves for her all over again.

I recognize myself in the old man. Hannibal and I share the same sickness in each other's minds. The Red Light Princess has gotten into our heads. Our blood grudge has tangled us better than lovers.

"You're not the only one out there haunted by her ghost. I see her too. But that does not mean that she is really there."

"You are wrong," he mutters.

"We've taken it too far," I say. "Our devotion is a disease. We turned her into a mad god. All those arms and legs... What does she do with them?"

"That's not my business. I am only her messenger." Hannibal's jaw clenches, "There is much I don't understand... Who knows what my poor girl has suffered in the grave? She says that I won't recognize her, that the other side has changed her. Being underground has toughened her skin into a bark. Black horns grew out from her skull. A tail drags behind her."

I shrug my shoulders, "Does it matter? She's all fiction, anyway. We'll never know who's really behind that mask."

"I know my little girl," the preacher says.

The pen rocks with a gust of wind. He's angry. His one hand looks exaggerated. It's ridged into a huge fist.

I grip at his sackcloth tunic, but he doesn't notice my touch. "Listen to me, old man. It's time to get your bearings. The 25's are out there looking for you. They want to sacrifice your body in the Mecha Beast Arena."

"I know all their moves before they make them," he scoffs.

"There are others. You have older, more dangerous enemies out there. My mother's back inside the walls. Sonya and my old pack are back in the No Go Zone. If you don't leave the separation barriers now, you won't last the night."

The preacher presses his stump against my neck and pins me against the bars, "You think I didn't pick up the scent of your pack when they stepped foot inside these walls, little cub?"

His elbow crushes my windpipe, "I have done you wrong, old man. Let me even our score. Leave this place before nightfall."

"You don't owe me a damn thing, little cub." The preacher draws me in, breath hot on my face. "The Red Light Princess is another matter. You'll pay back for every bone you stole. We'll start slowly: cut your fingers at the first bend and then move on to the next row of knuckles. Bit by bit, until I snap the wrist. Then you'll open wide for me and watch me rip out that tongue of yours. Fair is fair."

"We have both done terrible things to each other. I'm giving you your life for the things I've done to you. It's not a bad deal. Take it!" I try to scream some sense into him. "I've had my fill of this game."

Hannibal lets me go and opens the door of the cage. "This is not a game. None of us are getting out of this one alive. I have waited a long time for this moment. Run and hide, little cub. This place is a wilderness, man-eaters roam everywhere. We'll have our moment you and me."

I crawl out of the pen and peer over the edge. A cold pang hits the pit of my stomach. There's nothing but darkness out there. I jump into the void and lose myself in the rooftops below.

Chapter Nineteen
Black Kiss

Noise roars from the skywalks. The Night of the Clean Hands rolls on. Dawn's still a couple of hours away.

I smash the glass with my elbow and break into the high-rise to avoid the traffic on the roofs. Light from the bonfires outside pulls back from the windows.

I'm on my hands and knees, scurrying like vermin, darting away from the light, hiding in the unlit patches of the penthouse.

But this is what I am made for: evasion, scudding and hiding, the cowards run. This is all I know.

It's always the same. Every mother fucker out there is looking to collect a debt. They all have some grievance. I'm not saying that they don't have good reason. One way or another this is all on me. Nobody here is innocent. We all played our parts. I know that better than most.

We're all on a chase, and there's no sole hunter. Every one of us is closing in on the other. And we all have to look behind our backs to avoid getting what's coming to us.

I run around trying to find a way out of the building. The back windows are barred. The elevator shoot and emergency exits have been sealed off with brick and mortar.

There's a large fountain at the foot of a double-ended staircase. A cloud of tadpoles blackens the water. The marble statue at the center has been picked clean of body parts. Only the overturned torso remains half-sunk in the water.

I look into the pool but can't see my reflection. The water ripples. Something blows bubbles below the surface.

My implants start buzzing. A scurry of movement spreads all around me. Shadows warp on the walls. Footsteps scrape and tack in the background. They swarm at me from all sides.

Two shots pop from above the stairs. I hear something metallic clanking on the ground. A couple of metal canisters roll under my feet. They're electromagnetic pulse grenades. My eyes go wide open. I cover my ears and brace myself just as they blow.

The EMP blast ripples through the atmosphere. A burst of energy sends my body spinning. The blast shocks my system. Everything goes out of focus. Senses don't pick up a thing. I knock against the wall.

I roll around, groaning. My magnetite implants are overheated. They leech off the magnetic waves of the explosion, and it feels like they're sucking on lightning. My insides are cooked, launchers and wires smoking like a roasted pig.

It takes a bit to recover my senses. I turn on my belly to cough out a wad of spittle. My head pounds. Cold sweat drenches under my pits. The hole in my shoulder throbs every time I get a fit of the shakes.

"What are you doing crawling around on the ground?" Sonya walks down from the staircase. "You've taken the whole rat thing a little too seriously. This can't be healthy."

"You're not worried about me, are you?" Smoke slips out from my mouth. "Let's get this over with. I know why you're here."

Morien walks on the edge of the fountain with his arms extended like on a tightrope, "You say that like it means something."

Loki bites at the water, trying to fish out the tadpoles. The albino's legs look like the shanks of a prizefighter. Its knees are knobby and muscled. The Doberman keeps looking back at me.

Sonya sinks behind her furs, "Do you remember the last night we saw each other, Kai?"

"I remember everything." I glare into her eyes. "It was on that Night of the Clean Hands."

The urge is natural; it comes easily. It's a thing of instinct. I want to turn back, slip into an alley, and run; survive somehow. I don't want to get what I got coming.

I scan them one by one, making sure their eyes are on me. My voice echoes throughout the empty room. "Three simple rules and we broke them all. Every debt is forgotten. Violence is forbidden. Death is outlawed."

Sonya's braids flop over her shoulders like tentacles, "We were just out looking for a new place to take shelter—out on the hunt for living space."

I've tried to forget that night, but can't help but remember everything. "That's right. The west wall of our old building had collapsed."

Sonya paces around the room; her furs double her natural size. "I sent you boys out to scout for a new home for us: some place we could squat and call our own. But there was no unclaimed land out there. Every bit of livable space had already been taken. There was nothing left to spare. If we wanted a place of our own, we would have to drive someone else out and take it from them.

"Bale found the perfect place: a three-bedroom duplex with easy access to the roofs. It even had a view of the canals. The family that lived there was small, mostly girls. They looked like easy prey. But those bitches fought us for every inch of their home. They were armed to the teeth and held the high ground. We never had a chance. They sent us running with our tails between our legs. "

"But we left our mark there," Morien smirks, "We made that building shake and left it smoking for days."

"It was all for nothing," I say, "We killed too many of the neighbors in the firefight. Broke the rules. We went too far. Hannibal was right to track us down that night and put us in chains. What happened to Bale was a tragedy."

Sonya stares at me from the corners of her eyes. "We did nothing wrong. This is our calling: our birthright. It is something in our blood. We are the new world barbarians. We spread the hard truth. Nobody really owns a thing."

"We are not innocent here..." I pull out my chest and try the voice one more time.

"Nobody is," she says.

"The princess was innocent."

Her face furrows with an angry vector of lines. "I was made to kneel at that old man's feet and beg."

"Not hard enough..." I want to hurt her, make her remember.

She slaps me across the face, her first touch after all this time, "That man was stone... My son was fearless. He fought for every single breath. Bale deserved better than being slaughtered like some cheap offering."

"I wanted to close my eyes, but the screens were everywhere..." I mutter. "Bale would have wanted me to man up to the moment."

Sonya pulls back into a patch of darkness. Her voice is unfeeling. She speaks in a monotone. "That old man made me watch my son get eaten alive. And you want to take my revenge from me?"

"We took it already. Hannibal is broken. We snatched his only daughter and did terrible things to her. That old man went crazy when we were done." I shake my head, feeling weak and unsteady. "You wanted your revenge and we gave it to you. But it was never enough. You wanted the girl to suffer for you!"

Slowly but surely, I realize that I'm not putting on a front for her anymore. I let myself go a while back. This is just me now. And I'm not sure I like what's left.

"I helped you tear that girl limb from limb. But the Red Light Princess didn't shake in your arms, did she? You weren't holding the knife. You didn't feel the crack of her bones. What else do you want from me?"

Her eyes are frozen over, glazed hard as ice, "Look at you shake? You never had the stomach for this business. Such a soft, spongy boy… It should have been you that died that night."

"But I made it," I shrug my shoulders, "Luck's on my side then. That's all a man needs."

"You owe me…" she says.

"We should stop pretending we're not all bad men. The princess deserves her revenge. Her father is right. This place is a wilderness. Man-eaters roam everywhere."

Morien flashes me his impish smile, "Kai was always a little sweet on that girl. He likes them cold, stiff and buried."

My mother throws her furs to the ground. Sonya's prosthetic tail snakes behind her. The mechanical skeleton looks reptilian, segmented and armored with lozenge-shaped metallic plates like scales.

She raises the tail and a sharp, steel stinger slices from the nib. The metal barb folds out into separate fragments, forming a three-pointed spear.

The stinger lunges at me and drills clean through my shoulder, "You stole her from me!"

Sonya's face turns blurry, a reception I just can't catch. My eyes go out of focus. She's losing definition and melting into the background.

The pain hits me, sharp and overwhelming. My implants burn. I double over and fall on the ground.

I take in mouthfuls of air, desperate for oxygen. The ground seems unsteady, like it's about to swallow me.

Blood pools under my belly. My face is streaked with it like war paint.

Something bubbles inside the fountain. The water smokes. Dead tadpoles float on the surface. Fire licked salamanders jump out and make a run for it.

The princess's head surfaces from the water. She smiles at me. A blood red snake slips out from between her lips and splashes into the water.

"Do you see that?" I mutter.

"What do you see?" Sonya's turned formless. I can't see her face. She's shades of color, black stripes over gold.

"It's her," I answer.

"What is it about this girl that drives all of you wild? I'm going to burn that mummy in the skywalks. Everyone in this place will see that she is nothing special, just a sack of old bones."

The princes steps out from the water. Her black pearls are slick and dripping. Ribs show through a tear under her breasts. She stretches out her stumps and reaches out for me.

The blood loss's got me weak. Every breath is labored. I'm shutting down. "What's happening?"

"This is the price. There is a cost for the things we have

done." Sonya's voice is an echo, a sonic reverb. "I'm doing you a favor. This city belches out nothing but bodies. Men have gone too long without the touch of the sun. This is no way to live."

Sonya holds my head in her lap, but all I can see is the princess's blackened face. "I gave birth to strong, strapping sons. You were different. When you stumbled out of my womb, I almost crushed your little body with my thighs.

"We have taken everything from each other. Consider us even."

The princess touches my lips with hers. She gives me a black kiss. I'm cold and shaking, slowly drifting off.

I call to her, but no sound comes.

Chapter Twenty
The Red Light Princess

Hannibal rode at the head of a procession of motorbikes. His clansmen revved their engines and left black tracks on the bridge.

We were being paraded on the skywalks to the crowd, a string of padlocked chains harnessed around our necks. I wasn't all there. The chains tightened their grip around my throat.

Crowds had gathered on the rooftops. Men with painted faces hooted from atop the buildings. Fans held up the princess's portrait from the windows.

I fought to breathe and to keep up with the pace of the march. The noise was everywhere and hit me like static.

The crowd boomed, booing from every direction. We got pelted with rocks and bottles. Bags filled with warm shit were flung from the upper tiers.

A roar went up in the skywalks and the mob surged. A wave of bodies crashed against us.

I tried to keep on my feet. They whaled at me with their knuckles and elbows. I kicked back at them, but they pulled at my chain. The noose tightened. My eyes bulged from their sockets. Pressure built in my skull. I wheezed for air.

Sonya rolled on the ground. The crowd ripped at her clothes, tearing out clumps of fur. Men stuck their hands between her thighs. They lopped off her braids and collected the trophies in a pile.

She shook her head and tugged at the padlock on her neck, baring her teeth, screaming. Her furs bled like a wounded animal.

A set of giant screens flashed on. Hannibal's face came into focus.

The old man swiped a microphone in front of the speakers, sending a high-pitched shriek across the Mecha Beast arena. The whole place stopped and the mob started backing away. His clansmen herded them into the stands.

Hannibal's teeth scratched at the foam cover of the microphone, "She is the light of this dark city: our victory over the sun!"

The clansmen carried her in an open-topped litter. Whores from the canals broke into a dance and shook their hips to the beat of the drummers. Little girls, dressed in red veils, lit a row of candles as she approached. The whistle of the fireworks overhead echoed through the Zone.

She was hidden under a series of veils. The fabric was teasing, translucent. Its ends ballooned and flapped, twisting at her feet.

That was the first time I saw her, when the old man tore the coverings off her body.

The spectators on the skywalks roared. I watched the mob on the streets topple over each other, trying to reach her. A round of stray bullets went off. Grown men fell on their knees and cried. The people screamed her name.

Everyone had heard her name, seen the graffiti and heard the stories. But few had the chance to catch her in the flesh. She had more than the attraction of celebrity. The Red Light Princess was something else: old divinity, the new celebrity.

She was short in real life, a puckered mouth pixie a few inches short of a dwarf. Her entire body was tattooed with a web of vines and flowers. She wore a wig made out of black pearls. The strands clacked and rippled with the wind.

The princess took off a featureless porcelain mask. Her eyes were glass. The girl was someplace else, far away in the midst of a pleasant high. She looked straight at the crowd, but seemed to see nothing at all. The Princess sighed and let out a trail of smoke from her lips.

Hannibal's pixilated face blurred at the edges of the screens. "Out there they say men cannot survive without the sun. But we have proven them wrong. We have something better. The Red Light Princess is all we need. There is no hunger when she can feed you from her breast. There is no pain that cannot be soothed by her touch. Is there any desire that her thighs cannot satisfy? Take comfort that she is here and you are not alone."

The princess looked him up and down, her eyes squinted. She cocked her head and backed away, unable to recognize the old man.

His voice boomed from the speakers. The old man whipped at the microphone's black chord. "The ancient codes have been broken. These barbarians have spilled blood on our sacred night. One man always dies so the rest of us don't have to. I give you tonight's sacrifice!"

The image on the screens lagged behind his lips, "They will remember that we offer mercy, no one else. They have taken many lives tonight. But we are not bloodthirsty. We demand only one in payment: one man to die and close tonight's show."

His clansmen plugged Bales' chest with the electrodes of

a stun gun. He bucked and kicked at them, fighting through the shock. They grabbed him by the arms and took him to the arena.

Morien tried to get on his feet but got knocked down. Sonya screamed. I remained still and did nothing. Better men lash out when cornered. I folded.

The No Go Zone rocked with the noise of the crowd. The Red Light Princess stared into the black sky and opened her mouth. She was lost in some other place, far away from this one.

Sonya dropped on her knees. She heaved, her ribs caving in and expanding. Her mouth was on the pavement. Saliva pooled from the sides of her mouth. My mother began to beg.

The fluorescent war paint on Bale's face glowed in the dark. A single black braid ran down to his tailbone. Each knot was tied with ribbons and bells. The bells jingled as he fell into the arena.

A pack of mechanized hyenas, glass eyes shining a bright red, sniffed the air and surrounded him.

I wanted to look away, but the instant replay was on every jumbotron in the No Go Zone.

Up on the skywalks, far enough from the ground, I could see the day begin to break, "Anything out there?"

Morien climbed the rungs of a utility pole, "Darkness below, nothing ahead. I can't see a damn thing."

"She will come. The sun is rising," Sonya said. "The girl is drawn to the light."

Sonya's hair was cropped close to her scalp. Spiked patches ran along the top of her skull. She had covered herself in a set of bed sheets we had stolen from a clothing line. Rubber ducks were printed on the fabric.

She was straddling the railing of the bridge, a single breast exposed. I took off my shirt and covered my mother's chest with it. "It's very late. You're tired. Sleep would do you good. Our business can wait. We don't have to do this tonight."

She swiveled her eyeballs at me, "My son is dead and more will keep him company."

"I think I got her," Morien yells from the utility pole, "Something's moving two levels below."

The Red Light Princess was midway across the bridge. The girl walked on her tiptoes, lingering on the warm spots of cement. Natural light dripped over her body. The flowers and vines tattooed on her skin came alive and seemed to feed from the sun.

She had the wet look of early withdrawal on her skin. Her breathing was shallow. Her fingertips were tobacco stained. She went past us without noticing that we were there.

I pulled at her arm and brought her back to reality. Her eyeballs were all pupils, black and flat as disks. The princess was stunned. She didn't understand what was really happening. She reached up and touched my chin, scraping the stubble, making sure I was real.

Sonya knelt down to her level, cupping the girl's cheeks in her hands. "What are you?"

The Princess pulled away out of instinct. She stared at us nervously, her eyes gradually filling with fear. The fog was lifting.

Sonya opened the princess's mouth, lifting her lips to inspect the gums and teeth. "This pigmy is just another fake idol."

I held on to the girl's body and raised her off the ground. Her sweat was on me. It splashed into my mouth.

She squirmed in my arms. The girl shook and tried to get loose. She whipped her head and her pearl wig went flying off the edge of the bridge.

The Princess screamed and fell against me, covering her bald head with her hands.

I didn't know what to do. She clung to me, hiding her face on my chest.

Morien caught a noose around her throat. She clawed desperately at the ground. Her nails chipped and left a powdery residue on the concrete.

Sonya opened her mouth again and slipped in a knife. The blade clanked against her teeth. My mother wedged her fingers inside, snapping the tongue and a string of nerves from the girl's throat.

The princess screamed. She made a horrible bubbling sound.

Sonya took the piece of meat and milked it in her palms. A squirt of blood splattered on the ground.

I leaned on the rails and let my head hang back. My skull pounded. Everything happened quickly. I could smell the piss and fear gushing out from her.

There was nowhere to go. But I needed to distance myself from what was happening around me. I closed my eyes for a moment and tried to recede into my mind.

My brother took the knife next. Morien had her thighs opened. I could no longer see her, only his naked back. Her porcelain mask rolled to my feet. I pocketed it for some reason.

When Morien was done, he came back with one of her hands as a trophy. He handed me the knife. My brother closed my fingers over the handle.

I took a step back, shaking my head.

"I'm not doing this alone!" He unbuckled my belt and

tried to unzip my pants.

Sonya ran her fingers over the girl's bald head. "She's nothing special. The people have to see that her legend is all a lie."

A cold pang ran down my spine. The knife trembled in my grip. I looked back at Sonya and swallowed a mouthful of saliva.

I pinned the princess's shoulders with my knees. She closed her eyes and turned her face. I hacked the knife at her wrist. A gush blood splattered on my face.

My stomach churned. The blade got stuck on the bone. I looked away and tugged the knife loose.

I started chopping like mad, trying to get it over with. The knife was slippery and I kept missing, hitting the blade on the concrete.

The princess's hand came off mangled. Digits were missing. Splintered bones poked out from the skin.

I couldn't let go of the knife. It was clutched close to my body. The imprint of the blade was painted red on my belly. I wiped it off and backed up against the railing, looking down at the other bridges stretched out underneath the skywalk.

My mother picked up the pieces of the princess. She placed the remains of the girl's hands one over the other. The tongue was curled beside them.

"It's all about the message," Sonya said, "Burn her for all of them to see."

I tossed the knife over the rail and volunteered. The princess's body shivered at my touch. I flung her over my shoulder. Her little legs paddled as if underwater.

A rat, fat and spotted, was balanced on the skywalks railing. Its feet gripped the metal tubes. The animal extended one paw carefully over the other. It jumped off and landed on another bridge below, losing itself in the web of construction.

I understood the rat's movements, its surefootedness, the purpose of its speed. The animal was exposed, out of its natural element. It wanted to scuttle and hide: keep to the low ground, creeping through cracks and tunnels, wayfaring through unused space, an underground that is all its own.

It was in the pit of my stomach, spreading through my bloodstream: the urge to flee and run off with my catch. It prickled up my spine. My fingers fidgeted. Eyes darted from side to side.

This was my shot: the chance to roam on my own, the clean break I wanted. This was my moment. It was clear what I had to do. The pull of my pack was strong, but the urge to roam is a thing of instinct. They would be after me, but I had to run. This wasn't just about me anymore.

The little princess hugged me tight. One arm covered her bald head. I looked at the slices of my knife on her skin, the bones that jutted from her wrists.

This girl was more than an idol. I could touch her with my own hands. It didn't matter if she wasn't anything like her legend. Her celebrity was different. The Red Light Princess meant something. She was real.

I jumped the bridge's railing and flung myself over the edge with the girl held tightly in my arms.

I crash-landed on the deck of a bridge below and followed the rat's trail. I ran to the nearest rooftop and jumped to the next. The sunlight got blotted above me. There was nothing but darkness the deeper I got into the megastructure.

My head clocked from side to side. I saw movement all around me. Lights flashed. Figures leaped from roofs and bridges, rappelling from the sides of the high-rises.

Footsteps raced behind me. The shadows cast on the

wall morphed into a black streak. They were coming after me. I took the princess in my arms and kept on jumping, climbing higher and higher up the skywalk system.

I was sure that I had lost them when I reached the summit. I whispered to the princess that we were safe. But she didn't answer back.

She looked beautiful dead, even all cut up and mangled. The girl's body, her shape were recognizable. Her brand was not lost.

But something had changed. There was more to her now. Her body didn't look entirely human. There was something alien about it. Her skin was a pale marble. The vines and rosebuds on her body roiled and bloomed, coming alive with the sun.

She wasn't something for my eyes alone. She had to be shared. This woman was part of the public domain. Everyone had to be given a chance to say goodbye to her.

I put her mask back on her face and hung her from the tallest skywalk for everybody to see.

The word had spread. A large crowd gathered to watch her hang. Thousands of men and women held up candles and burned incense. Monks in saffron-colored robes rocked and chanted, leading the prayer.

On the higher floors, housewives peeked from their windows. Gawkers, commuters and curiosity seekers were packed against the railings of the upper walkways. Whores went out on their balconies, gossiping between puffs of smoke.

I was in the mix, blending with the mourners, fighting for space like the other spectators, trying to get a good view, owed my fair share of the spectacle.

I wake up gasping for air. My lungs feel punched. I'm conscious, but too weak to move.

I inhale air through my nostrils, taking lungfuls in quick, desperate snorts. My tongue presses against the balled-up rag stuffed inside my mouth. I'm hogtied, my arms and legs duct-taped behind my back.

The crowd out there roars. Their noise charges up the atmosphere with an electric vibe. Its static sprays against me like rainwater. I want to open my mouth and feel it spark against my tongue.

I'm back on street level. The roads are littered with trash dumped from the skywalks and roofs.

My old pack is gone. They've left me at the foot of the Mecha Beast Arena wrapped like a present, choking on the balled-up rag stuffed inside my mouth.

Someone's coming up on me. My implants bite at my bone. They pulse and heat up as she gets closer.

Two spotlights blaze down at me. Buzzards fly circles over my body. The spider-like eyes of their cameras zoom in.

Mercury looks down on me from the barrel of a six shooter, "Don't look at me like that. I warned you. You always knew it was gonna end this way."

Chapter Twenty One
Mecha Beast Wars

Mercury pushes the barrel of her gun on the nape of my neck, "Move."

We step into the elevator, flanked by her drones. The buzzard's lenses slot out. They keep a close eye on me.

She pulls on the lever, and a red bulb flashes over our heads. The cargo elevator jerks up the exterior of the building and climbs up to the arena.

The elevator lurches to the rooftop. It screeches to a stop at a metallic platform at the base of the ring. Mercury slides open the mesh wire screens and orders me out from the car.

The Mecha Beast arena spread out in front of me. It's huge. The arena takes up an entire city block. A crooked network of metal stands are cramped on every rooftop. Bonfires burn in the background.

The ring is in the middle of the structure. The rooftop has been caged behind a chain link dome. A ring of spotlights crown the top of the arena.

There's a series of rungs on the side of the chain link dome. Black and red electrical wires run down the crosspieces and connect to the spotlights. We climb up the ladder and come to the top of the ring. The wind whips back my rattail.

My implants buzz like mad. The stands rock with noise. Spectators thump their feet on the nosebleed seats. Shirtless thugs hoot and throw bottles. A fight breaks out on the queue to the portable toilets. Free jumpers hop around, building to building, trying to find seats closer to the ring.

Jumbotrons hangs from these thick, black cables anchored to the skywalks. They play a live feed from the ring.

Johnnie Manila's face flashes on the screens. He's in one of the private boxes that border the fighting ring. It's been decked out with aluminum palm trees and disco balls. Waitresses in feathered headdresses do the rounds with bottles of bubbly. An open bar runs in the background.

Camera men take shots of the clan chiefs and triad bosses in their skyboxes. They are the men that run the No Go Zone. The bosses bounce girlies on their laps and clap at the action on the screens. Their foot-soldiers and security detail roam in the background.

Manila's barracuda grin is half-covered by the microphone, "Six straight hours of blood and glory and now only two remain. These Mecha Beasts, half wild instinct, half calculated killing machine, will face each other in a match to the death!"

The spotlights turn on and light up the ring. He gets on his feet, whipping the microphone's chord, "Making his debut appearance on this Night of the Clean Hands is the six-wheeled, three-speed sensation, a cold-blooded monster with a circular buzz saw that speeds up to three thousand RPM, the challenger tonight, Crock the Ripper!"

The crocodile rolls into the arena with a cloud of smoke shooting from its exhaust. Its body is covered in a chassis of pipes and tubing. Three sets of wheels are attached to the axles running under its belly. The reptile's tail swings behind it. The buzz saw running at its end screeches and throws off sparks.

"But is it up for the challenge?" Manila's voice booms

across the rooftops. "It is up against a living legend. At three hundred pounds of metal and over five hundred pounds of muscle, this mechanized beast has ripped and rampaged his way to the top of the pack for two years in a row. He is going for the record tonight. The big daddy of them all, ladies and gentleman, Otto the Shock Bear!"

The crowd goes wild as Otto steps into the ring. The bear feeds off the attention. He starts running laps around the roof, making sure the cameras catch him from every angle. Otto gets up on his hind legs, raises his paws into the air and roars.

The crowd loves him. He whips them up, getting them good and riled. They wave his banners and shout his name. The bear has them right where he wants them.

A bell goes off and the fight begins. The crock revs up its motor and burns rubber. It zips right at its opponent. The reptile hits the breaks and turns the wheels just as it is about to hit. It crashes against the bear with the side of its chassis, knocking the champ down.

Crock the Ripper makes a roundabout-like turn and guns it, trying to run over the bear while he's still down. The bear looks stunned. He's having trouble getting back on his feet. But he manages to shake off the confusion and rolls away just in time.

The Mecha Beasts circle each other. Otto crouches on all fours, swiping at the crock to keep it back. The reptile attempts to inch closer. Its jaws snap, trying to get close enough to bite.

Crock the Ripper lunges at the champ and takes a hold of its front leg. The reptile's buzz saw rips into the bear's armor and draws blood.

Spectators rush in a wave to the lower seats, pushing

themselves against the mesh wire fence that borders the stands. They topple over each other and climb up the barrier for a better view.

Otto manages to break the crock's hold. He gets up on his hind legs and lunges on top of the crocodile, holding on tight to the tail to keep the saw away.

Crock the Ripper wheels around wildly, trying to shake off the bear. It crashes against the fence and turns over.

The bear pins the reptile down and takes a chomp right out of its belly. He has a mouthful of meat, rubber, and metal sparking up against his electric muzzle.

Johnnie Manila grips the stem of his microphone, voice surging, "Otto the Shock Bear has broken the record. Behold, our champion!"

The crowd jumps to their feet, screaming. Stray bullets go off in every direction. Free jumpers spin over the roofs. Topless girls throw their bras overboard.

A swarm of buzzards circle around me. Their cameras zoom in on me. My face flashes and dissolves on the public screens.

"One man always dies so the rest of us don't have to." Johnnie Manila's voice spreads out through the sky. "Tonight's sacrifice is brought to you Courtesy of the 25's of District Five. Otto the Shock Bear gets one more kill! Are you up for it, big boy?"

The bear beats against the chain link fence and snarls at the camera. He's a three-time champion. The bear's no noob. He knows how to play his part.

Mercury tears the strip of duct tape from my lips. "Are you ready, handsome?"

"No." I mutter, "I don't think so."

She opens the hatch into the ring, "This show is almost

over, Kai. All you have to do is give the crowd what they want. You got nothing to do but die."

I stare at the crowds in the stands of the arena, "Look at them out there. The Night of the Clean Hands is a fool's game. We are all getting played."

"I know it." She digs her metallic heel into my spine and kicks me into the ring.

Chapter Twenty Two
The Sacrifice

I land on my ass. My body splashes into a puddle of the crocodile's blood. It speckles across my eyes. The spotlights aim straight at me, hot and blinding.

The bear catches my scent. His fur bristles, forming a sharp crown of bleached spikes across his back. He scratches the ground and charges at me.

My heart beats against my chest. Instinct kicks in. I run over to the fence and start climbing the chain links to get away from the bear.

The crowd boos at me. They whistle from the back of the stands, throwing bottles, cans and bags filled with piss against the cage.

Otto sits back on his haunches. His tongue is out and unrolled, saliva sizzling on his muzzle. He watches me squirm.

The bear gets up on his hinds. He looks huge. The animal's fur is thick and matted. His chest is covered in a gleaming armor. He jumps and swipes his claws at me. They dig deep into my back. I scream and drop back to the ground with a thud.

Otto comes for me. He thinks he's going for the kill. I jump on my feet, front flip over the Mecha Beast, and land behind him.

I stab my crampons on bear's hind leg, but get caught in a clump of his fur. The bear turns back. His muzzle goes straight for me.

I grab on to the metal to push it back, but the electric blast sends me flying across the ring.

On the ground. Muscles contracting. Going into spasms. Magnetite implants heat up, red as coals. They burn through my skin.

I get up and spit out a wad of blood off the side of the ring. Black spots form around my eyes. I have to shake my head a couple of times to get my sight back.

The bear snarls, charging at me with a vengeance. I sidestep around him, managing to dodge every one of his swipes. I have to be careful. There's cooked body parts strewn all over the ring.

Adrenaline boosts through my veins. I'm all one instinct. I want to escape. Cut and run. There is nowhere for me to go but outside. I jump over the bear and climb back to the chain link dome. I kick start my talons and cut a hole through the fence.

I crawl out of the dome on all fours. On bottom feeder level, suctioned to the chain link like a roach. Out of sight. Ducking the spotlights.

I dodge an incoming bottle and try to quicken my pace, but my talons keep slipping. I can't get a sure footing. The spikes are of no use. Too many blades are missing. They can't get a good hold.

My implants are fried, but still work. I feel the vibrations coming before it happens. The whole ring starts shaking. A couple of beams snap and collapse. The shock bear's climbing outside of the ring. His weight is taking the whole structure down.

The impact hits me like a sledgehammer. It pounds my body and lifts me off the ground. I'm suspended and thrown over the edge of the ring.

Awareness catches me, and I manage to hold on to one of the rungs on the side of the cage. My arms tremble and can barely support my own bodyweight. I don't want to look down, but I do it anyway.

I plant my crampons on the chain link and start climbing back up, but the ring is coming apart as I go. The ceiling is collapsing into the ground. Slabs of concrete hurl down to the streets. Black wires whip at me from the broken spotlights.

The Shock Bear mewls desperately, stuck in a tangle of metal and concrete.

I climb back up on the platform and head for the cargo elevator.

Mercury blocks my path. She's got her gun in a double-handed grip. One eye, black and unblinking, has me in her sights.

I take my chances and tackle her. My teeth bite into her shoulder blade. I push her into the elevator car, slamming her against the back of the cage.

She bucks against me, and I stumble back. Her six-shooter points between my eyes.

I kick her feet in with my gnarled crampons. She goes down in a slam.

We roll on the ground. I struggle to take the gun from her. She keeps firing the revolver, keeping me unsteadied with the recoil. I bash my forehead against her nose, pry the six-shooter from her hands, and toss it outside the elevator.

Mercury crawls on her hands and knees, slithering out of the cabin, reaching for her gun.

I close the sliding door, clamping her wrist against the frame of the elevator. My hand goes for the elevator's lever. Her eyes widen and she screams, "No!"

I pull the lever. A bulb flashes over my head. The lift jerks loose and rushes down the shaft.

Mercury crashes against the roof of the cabin. Her hand tears off in a snap. Blood sprays on my face.

The elevator shoots into the streets. Sparks flare from the pulleys and suspension rope. I grab onto the handlebars and brace myself until we hit solid ground.

Mercury's covered with a slick film of blood. She still has the feel of her ghost fingers. The woman touches her stump, trying to find her lost hand, gripping at something that's no longer there.

I crouch down and meet her eyes, "I expect I'll be seeing you again. Everybody wants their revenge. I knew there would be something special between us."

Mercury chews on her lips with her jade teeth and glares back at me with thoughts of violence. Her pupils swell; black ink roils in her eyeballs. "It's almost dawn. The Night of the Clean Hands will be over soon. Every man out there will be on his own."

I run out into the street, find a fire escape and climb up to the roofs.

The southern skywalk system spreads ahead of me. I can see the Venus Horn looming in the horizon. It is half covered in a cloud of smog. The deck hovers at the top of a winding, concrete hive.

I dive off the roof with a cold pang running down my spine. I can't help it. I start sweating it. Paranoia sets in. I get second thoughts in mid-air, but there is no way to go back now.

Chapter Twenty Three
The Venus Horn

The climb's a hard one. I scale higher and higher up the super structure, bouncing from one skywalk to the next.

My body's not with me. Balance is off. I've got no footing. My reflexes are getting slow. I stumble around and miss my marks. This is getting hairy. My implants feel like they're purring at me. I'm sweating cold and shaking.

I look down at the height of the drop, but can't see bottom, only darkness. I get dizzy. My eyes blur at the edges. Things spin around. I come close to crashing splat to the pavement.

My body is exhausted. But I have no choice. I have to will myself to keep moving. I know it already. If I stop, I'll collapse and tumble down.

I manage to pull myself up on the next bridge. The deck is empty—not a soul on it. All I can hear is my talons screeching on the concrete.

My eyes dart from side to side. The silence feels odd on a night like this. It's suspicious. I cannot trust this moment.

I blast an EMP and scan the surroundings to catch anything creeping up on me, coming at me from my blind spots. But nothing's moving out there. It's just my paranoia, again. I've never been able to shake it off. The thing sticks with me. Bad habits always do.

It starts drizzling. The drops splash on me and slime

down my cheek. My tongue is dry. I open my mouth wide, eager to have a drink. I slurp at the droplets, but gag as soon as I swallow.

It's blood. The taste is thick and metallic. I purge it out, unable to keep it inside. More of it rains down on me. The blood splatters everywhere. My face gets slick with it.

I look up, and there's a clutch of dead girls hanging from the top of a utility pole.

The utility pole's trunk is covered in a hard bark of grime. Bodies hang from a canopy of black power cables. This thing looks like a tree blooming fresh corpses.

The girls are all made up. They're in full club gear: neon body paint, diamond-shaped pasties, furs and stockings clamped together with metallic, pincer-like garters.

I can smell it off them: the sugary rot. They've already started to turn. Their extremities are bruised with black and blue patches of settled blood. They have probably been out here since night fell.

They are all cut up, scars on the insides of their thighs, missing arms, legs, and toes. But each body is different. No single corpse has the same combination of amputations.

I climb up the rungs of the utility pole and start rifling through the bodies. The shakes come back again. I pull one corpse and then toss it aside to check the next. But Ana Kwong is not here with them.

These poor girls are just bad impersonators. They look cheap, really. There's nothing special about them. They are just reaching out to get noticed. They don't want to be invisible anymore. They don't want to get lost in crowds.

But these casualties will barely break through the media cycle. The micro blogs will only mention them in passing. They will never make it to the jumbotrons. For all their effort at suicide, these girls don't measure up.

I move up the different levels, quickening my pace, pushing my body, getting closer to the summit of the skywalk system. The Venus Horn is only a few stories above me.

I reach the observation deck and take a breath of cold air. The separation barriers spread all around me. I can see every part of the No Go Zone from up here.

The observation deck is stocked with chrome-plated binoculars. They were originally coin-operated, but the telescopes had been picked and prodded. We tore out their insides and disabled the token mechanisms, liberating the machines, recalibrating them for free public consumption.

A ring of broken columns line the edge of the balcony like molars.

Ana Kwong looks through one of the telescopes. The boy's naked back is turned to me.

He's all dolled up. His body has been freshly tattooed with an exquisite design of thorned vines and flowers. He's small, a few inches short of a dwarf. Everybody's been right. The boy is something special. He looks just like her. The black pearls on his head clack with the wind.

I go back on all fours, flat on my belly, and hide behind one of the broken columns.

My body throbs all over. I've got the shakes like a quake. Knees buckle. I can barely keep myself going because of the pain.

Drones fly around the building. They beam their spotlights at the balcony. A huge crowd of onlookers has gathered on the skywalks and is looking down at us. More people crowd the roofs around the block. They peep out the windows and huddle on the fire escapes. It feels like the entire No Go Zone is watching.

Ana Kwong sits on the edge of the balcony. The boy slips his legs over the edge. His little feet paddle. He can't help but smile, toying with idea of the drop below.

I smell the coriander and vanilla coming off his skin. His sisters were something else. But he's perfect. Nobody's ever played the princess like him.

He's got his stumps crossed over his chest to brace against the cold. His pelvic bone pops from his hips, framing a nest of closely cropped pubic hair. He spits out a coin from his mouth, and it tumbles down to the streets.

The monks scrub him down with wet rags and rubbing alcohol. They cleanse his body for the ritual. One of them polishes every one of the pearls on his wig. The monks want him fresh and looking spanking new. He has to be perfect for the fall.

Hannibal prays on his knees. He grips the nib of his stump hard, clamping it with his one good hand, the knuckles white with the pressure.

The preacher gets off the ground and walks to the boy's side, "Are you scared?"

The boy turns his head, eyes black and flat as disks. His mouth moves, but no sound comes out. He's high as hell. Just like her.

Hannibal smiles at him. His voice is kind, calming. He pulls the noose over the boy's head and fastens it.

"The body is an altar for sacrifice. Each piece is cheap," the preacher says.

The boy closes his eyes as the mask approaches him. He shivers when the cold porcelain touches his skin.

"The princess is almost here. I can feel it." Hannibal looks down from the balcony. "She is just underneath us now.

All she needs is the signal: one last flare to show her the way home."

His eyes are full of love and wonder. It's something insane. But I recognize what I see. It's something we share: an old obsession, a shared guilt that we can never leave behind, the same incurable disease.

I know this is all crazy. This is just a game in the old man's head. The princess is dead. But I can't help it. It comes naturally to me. I'm excited to see her again.

The crowd outside starts roaring. They're packed against the railings of the skywalks, hooting and cheering. Some go overboard and drop down into the pavement. The noise is everywhere and hits me like static.

I want to close my eyes as the boy jumps off the balcony, but the screens are everywhere. The footage plays in a constant loop. There's no hiding from it.

I swallow hard, man up to the moment, and dive in after him.

Live footage on the public screens shows him waving at crowds as he falls. The spotlights lose him. The boy drops fast, his body getting lost in the darkness.

I try to pick up speed, swoop in and catch him in my arms. But the closer I get to him, the faster he pulls away. I stretch out my hand to him, but he won't take it. He drops like a stone. It's too late. The boy is out of my reach.

My implants pick it up before it happens. They feel the rope tense and her neck break. Ana's body blows from side to side with the wind.

The crowds on the roofs start roaring. The noise spreads everywhere. It reverbs off the high-rises, howls through the streets and alleyways.

I close my eyes and let my body drop in a free fall.

Chapter Twenty Four
Lair of Bones

I bounce off the rails of a fire escape and land on top of an abandoned office tower four stories down.

The air gets knocked out of me. Breathing is painful. More than one of my ribs breaks. That nasty wound on my shoulder feels tender again.

I roll over and crawl to the edge of the roof. The spotlights shines on her body. It looks tiny from way down here. The porcelain mask glints in the darkness. She looks just like her.

A huge crowd has gathered underneath the body. They pile over each other, burning candles and trashcan pyres. The crowds jam-pack against the edge of the skywalks and rooftops. Free jumpers fly around the body, trying to reach out and touch her feet.

I turn my back on the hanging Venus and jump to the cluster of skywalks ahead.

Traffic is heavy. The bridges are crowded with commuters, sunken-eyed club kids and stragglers left over from the festival. Some of them are still trying to keep the party going. I'm in the mix, pushing them out of the way, trying to get ahead of the crowd.

I have to move quickly. My old pack is still out there. They won't let go of our old blood grudge. The princess is in danger. I have to get to her first.

I owe that girl everything. It's about time I pay off my debts.

My implants start buzzing again, hot as coals. I'm being followed.

Something trails me. It feels like it's matching the beat of my step, shadowing me, every move. I look over the rails.

A monstrous wing beats under the skywalk. The elastic membrane's tattooed with an arabesque of vines, thorns and rosebuds.

My body goes cold. I pick up my pace and make the jump to the rooftops on the neighboring block.

I hit the roof rolling on my elbows. Barbeque smoke exhausts from the lower floors and gathers above me. My body keeps low to the ground. I'm on my hands and knees, scurrying like vermin, gaining speed for my next jump.

I land on a window ledge and look over my shoulder to see if that thing is still on to me.

It's still there, moving around in the dark. The thing is big and trying to hide behind a high-rise. Its black tail coils around the base of the tower.

The streets get emptier the closer I get to the Mausoleum of the Red Light Princess. The ground is littered with dead bats, a few of them still alive. The animals roll and fight on the pavement.

The mausoleum's dome reflects the bonfires on the skywalks. It looks overheated, like the marble will burn to the touch. The gates are unlocked and swung open.

I get on all fours and creep inside, keeping low, hugging the walls. My hands crunch on broken glass and my knees scrape against rubble. I stick to the spaces reserved for crawling, lowborn things.

Morien is mounted on the princess's casket. He pops

the lid with one crack of his crowbar. The bulletproof panes dislodge from the frame.

Sonya looks over the mummy. Her furs bristle at her back.

Loki catches my scent and starts to bark.

I try to sidle out of there. My legs inch backwards. I can't help but blush, feeling found out. I'm a kid again caught playing with a dead rat.

My mother's eyes swivel at me, "Get off your knees, Kai."

I get on my feet and inch closer to her. The dented spikes on my crampons screech on the floor. "You don't need the trophy. She's just plastic and bones."

"I'm here for what you stole from me." Sonya sinks into her furs, her own body lost in the hide. "This girl is mine. She's bait to draw the preacher to me. I'm going to watch them both burn."

She runs her fingers over the princess's mask. The porcelain reflects the red dome.

The mummy looks fragile to the touch. Her ribs and pelvic bone poke out from underneath the flesh-toned zentai.

"You don't understand," I say, "This girl is special."

Morien tosses the crowbar and jumps down from the casket, "Kai's always been sweet on this girl. Maybe, he's turned believer."

"We have a new preacher in town. Another madman clinging to his idol. My poor son, you went down the wrong road." Sonya's nails claw the princess's mask and slide off the porcelain. "I'm going to snatch this mask off her face and show you there's nothing behind it."

The mausoleum shakes. A loud thump comes from the dome, sending a shockwave through the crypt. Something big lands over our heads.

I look up at the ceiling and swallow an electric prickle of anxiety. "Can you feel it? She's here."

"He's gone insane," Morien says, "There's nothing out there."

"She's going to hunt us down," I mutter, "That girl deserves her revenge."

Hannibal steps into the burial chamber. His tunic is torn to rags. The old man's chest is zippered with scar tissue. He holds a double-edged axe with his one good hand.

"We got them right where we want them, my little princess." The preacher's milky eyes sweep the room. "The she-wolf and her bloodthirsty cubs in their lair of bones."

A black tail slithers through the gates. The nib probes the ground. It's ridged with a set of deformed plates and shingled with black scales.

I don't trust what I see, but the thing feels real just the same. I want to reach out and touch her tail.

"She has tunneled out from her grave," Hannibal says. "The digging was hard. Our girl is hungry. Her tripe is churning."

Every stitch on Morien's arms pops loose. The skin begins to slit open. The scythes slide out with a slow drip of blood. He jumps at the preacher.

Hannibal brings the axe down on my brother's head. It explodes in a splatter of blood, brain matter and chips of bone. The old man forces the blade off the skull with his heel.

Sonya' stinger springs out from her prosthetic tail. She drives the iron trident into Hannibal's face. The center prong drills into his forehead. The spikes on the sides pop both eyeballs.

Hannibal teeters, unsteadily. He's bleeding badly. Shaking. His knees begin to give. But he finds his footing and smiles back at Sonya. He pulls the stinger off his face, brings his axe down, and lops off both her hands.

Sonya tries to scream, but the preacher lunges at her, covering her groans with a kiss. They embrace, almost passionately, bucking and grunting, splashing in their sweat. He comes off her holding half of her tongue clamped between his teeth.

The dome starts shaking again. The thing on top of it is angry. It's riled and beating against the marble. A webbed alien claw bursts through the gates of the crypt and scratch marks the ground.

Its nails spread out and reach for me. I try to backtrack, but it slices at my leg and knocks me down.

I look up at the ceiling. Cracks break on the marble. The red dome comes crashing down on us. Broken stones smash on the ground. Bricks start coming loose. The walls of the mausoleum tumble apart in a tide. A cloud of dust blinds me. All I can hear is the thing outside screeching.

Chapter Twenty Five
The Burial

The atmosphere's choked. I take mouthfuls of hot ash. There's a sharp pain in my ribs. I breathe with a wheeze. The shock has me sweating cold. My focus is off. I stumble over the rubble with no idea where I'm going.

I walk around the ruins, kicking loose fragments of the red dome.

Morien's body lies buried under a pile of bricks. Loki is grey with the debris. It's licking at Morien's heels. The albino whimpers and pants, running circles around the body. It's desperate, nudging him with its paws, nibbling at his clothes with its front teeth.

Hannibal and Sonya lie one on top of the other. Their bodies cradled in each other's arms.

The princess's casket lies overturned on the ground, its underside crumpled. Her mummy is tossed over. The porcelain mask is fissured into two pieces over her face.

My fingers run through the crack. I try to remove the ceramic, but it has fused into her flesh.

I pick up the Red Light Princess in my arms and take off. Her little body is flimsy, about to blow away with the breeze.

The Red Light Princess has to be given a proper burial. She has been on display long enough. This girl's been pimped for the last time.

Loki trails close behind me. The dog howls and looks up

at me with sad, pink eyes.

I try to ignore it, but the dog barks at my back. A soft whine strains from its throat. The albino presses its wet nose on the bite mark on my leg and licks at the wound.

"What is it that you want?" I ask.

Loki lowers its head. The albino rests on its hind legs. Its shoulders tent under the white fur.

"Look…." I crouch down to the animal's eye level, sharing its same line of vision. "I know it. We understand each other. We're all alone. You and I are all that's left of our pack."

The dog crawls on its belly and nuzzles my feet. We recognize something in each other, a shared history that we can never leave behind, the stink of an old, familiar scent. The pull of the pack is strong.

"You better get a move on it if you're coming with me."

We head down an underpass. Wet clothes drip from a chain of electrical cords. Transients down here collect their belongings in plastic bags, swiping their guns at anything that moves. Families huddle around cook fires. They boil rice out of aluminum cans.

Hawkers sell their wares in the back. An old man shows off a stack of motherboards. Two identical brothers push stolen electronic gear. Barefoot children scuttle about offering sweet deals on consoles and pirated software. Women keep to the margins, warming themselves by the cook-fires.

I find a patch of wet earth and start digging. My hands are caked in mud. I'm making a mess and splattering it everywhere.

I start to draw a crowd. The people whisper and point at the body. Some drop to their knees and pray. Others light candles. A young woman plops on the ground, her daughter clinging around her neck, and moves the dirt with her bare hands. A few of the hawkers bring shovels. The transients help dig with blackened tin cans.

I lay the Red Light Princess softly into the ground, easing her into her grave. The blank mask over her face is riddled with new cracks. It is crumbling to pieces.

My lips touch the porcelain.

I try to mutter a prayer for the princess, but I don't know how to comfort her. I'm tired of trying and coming up short. Instead, I just say goodbye.

Back on the skywalks, my talons try to keep their grip on the edge of the deck.

I'm tired but can't help the rush of adrenaline that traces in my veins. Everything before this moment is something distant and edged with static. I feel hot and alive. A smile tears at my face.

Loki's on his haunches beside me, his tongue unrolled from the side of his muzzle.

Day is breaking. The sunlight licks at the rooftops but never filters down to the streets. My implants start buzzing. They're hot and urgent. Loki's on a hair trigger, fur bristled and already snarling.

I look over my shoulder and smile.

Mercury lurks in an unlit patch of the bridge. She's bound her stump with a rag. Her one good hand grips at the handle of her six shooter. She's making up ground and coming after me.

Our eyes meet. I wave my hand in her direction. An electric spasm runs down my spine. The chase is on again.

I dive off the skywalk and drop down to the roofs, scuffing and rolling, losing myself in the twisted grid orbiting the slums.

My implants shoot an electromagnetic pulse from my launchers. The wave sweeps over the buildings and reaches out to the separation barriers. I feel the warmth baking the stones on the other side of the walls. The magnetic fields out there are revved with explosive outbursts of energy. I try to get a feel of what's outside.

I've always wanted to see what is on the other side. Chase the sun, follow the spring and roll east.

Acknowledgments

A special thanks to my editor, Mara Hodges, and the team at Montag Press, for helping me make this novel readable, and bring *the Red Light Princess* to life.

Author Bio

James W. Bodden is a writer living in Tegucigalpa, Hondu-ras. In addition to writing fiction, James has hunted for fresh corpses as a crime beat reporter, and for UFOs as the host of a paranormal radio show. *The Red Light Princess* is his debut novel. You can follow James's tweets @jwbodden.

www.ingramcontent.com/pod-product-compliance
Lightning Source LLC
Chambersburg PA
CBHW030129260626
47156CB00008B/2866